DEDICATION

To my mother, the heroine of every chapter of my life.

Your world was built around the people you loved.
You gave it all without hesitation.
Every step you took, every sacrifice you made,
was for your family's dreams and our tomorrow. You
gave, not for praise, but because love was your
instinct, your compass and your calling.

With courage stitched into your every breath,
you stood unshaken. Your determination became our
foundation. Your selflessness became our hope.
Your strength and devotion became our guide.

This story, and every story I will ever tell,
carries pieces of your relentless and heroic heart.

*For all the dust you swept from our path
and all the love you planted in its place,*

**I dedicate this book to you Mama, the reason dust
can twirl into possibility. You are my hero, forever!**

Athena: Swirls of Unsettled Dust

Chapter 1: Lekka, Samos, Greece

The incredible night sky over Lekka shimmered like a velvet cloth stitched with thousands of brilliant silver threads. Athena liked to think that each star was a tiny sailboat, gliding across the heavens while ferrying dreams between magical islands in the sky. Often, when she couldn't sleep, she would close her eyes and sail away from their little stone house, into the marvel of Lekka's sky. She floated while bouncing off clouds, away from the heavy sounds that cracked the night like splitting wood. Tonight was one of those nights.

Athena pressed her face against the top of Katerina's back. The child was only six. Many called her the bony one. Her thick brown hair covered the front of Athena's face like a wet blanket soaked with the smell of seawater. Her ribs fluttered beneath Athena's hand like a bird trapped under glass.

Athena squeezed her eyes shut and let her mind take flight. Lekka, she thought, was the most beautiful place in the whole world. She often told her siblings stories, saying that the gods had once kissed the mountains of Lekka and taught the olive trees to dance in the wind. In the mornings, when the sun spilled over the hilltops, everything turned to gold. The morning dew revealed the glimmer in every stone wall, from the broken down homes to the crooked rooftop tiles in the village. Even the dusty goat paths marked with winding prints, shone bright with every sunrise as if releasing the luster of hidden jewels. Athena used to run barefoot along those paths, laughing and singing into Lekka's wind.

The two thin mattresses had been pushed together at one end, forming a long, makeshift bed that creaked and sagged beneath them like a tired raft, struggling to stay afloat. Eight of them lay crammed together, lying side by side, in a long horizontal line up, heads against the cold stone wall, feet spilling over the other edge. They were packed so tightly that when one stirred, a ripple spread across the others like a wave across still water. Next to Eleni, Christina's teeth clicked a soft, rhythmic sound like pebbles rattling in a tin. Athena could tell that she was trying to stop, biting her lips and holding her breath, but fear made Christina's body tremble all the same. Little Anna let out another whimper, not loud, just a broken little bird sound. Maritza, who was only nine, already knew too much. She pulled Anna close against her chest and rubbed her back in slow circles. At the far end of the aligned mattresses, Aphrodite, the oldest sibling at seventeen, lay stiff and silent, her fingers clenched in the worn blanket.

Athena could see Aphrodite's lips moving slightly, whispering something, praying, or perhaps just wishing herself somewhere else. A sharp growl, loud and aching, broke the heavy stillness. It was not a voice, nor an animal, but someone's stomach. It could have been Katerina's, or Athena's, or all of theirs. Athena pressed her hand over her belly to smother the next grumble. They knew the walls were thin. They could hear everything, even when they tried not to. They blocked their ears with their little hands. The usual sounds, the heavy thud of boots, the sharp crack of a quickly swallowed blow, and muffled cries were there tonight too. They all knew to be quiet because if Father heard, if he thought they were awake, he might come in, and that was worse than hunger.

At the end of the first mattress by the cracked window, Pavlos lay perfectly still. Even in his sleep, his fists were clenched so tightly that his nails dug deep into his palms, leaving angry half moon indentations. He was Father's pride, the only boy and the only one that really mattered. He was nine, with a crown of messy curls and wide hazel eyes. "Strong boy," Father called him. "My lion." Athena sometimes wondered if Pavlos felt the weight of Father's pride the way they all felt Father's wrath. Maybe he carried it like a heavy coat he couldn't take off, even when the summer sun burned Samos.

She squeezed her eyes shut and ran through the names again, *Aphrodite, Eleni, Christina, Maritza, Pavlos, Katerina, Anna,* and herself, *Athena,* eight children, lined up like beads on a fraying string. There had been another, Andreanna who was born just nine months after Athena. She died when she was only two. Some said she was so beautiful that Mother had to cover her face on the way to church for fear of the evil eye. Mother believed in the evil eye. They all did. She said that's what got Andreanna in the end.

Another sound seeped through the thin wall, a slap, then a stifled gasp. It was never loud. Mother knew better than to be loud. The mattress shuddered as Christina shook harder, her little body jerking. Athena reached out and found her sister's hand. It was trembling, slick with sweat, but the grip was fierce and desperate. Athena's chest ached with the force of it. "Shh," she breathed into the dark, no louder than the soft hiss of the wind through the fig trees outside.

Athena thought about the narrow streets of Lekka and the winding lazy rivers of rain between the houses. The cobblestones were uneven, worn smooth by generations of footsteps. When it rained, puddles formed in the dips of the winding roads. They were perfect for sailing little paper boats. Athena often raced her brother Pavlos down those streets, laughing wholeheartedly, until *Yiaya* would scold them from her doorstep while waving her wooden spoon. Her thoughts were thin blankets against the night, barely enough to keep out the cold and the terror. She heard a low moan filtered through the wall, followed by a heavy, dragging sound. Maybe Mother had fallen. Maybe she was getting up again. Athena pictured the sun dappled fields outside the village, where wild thyme grew in thick carpets and bees hummed lazily among the wildflowers. In her imagination, she ran barefoot across the warm earth, the sun hot on her hair and the air full of the sweet scent of honey.

They heard another creak, softer and slower this time. They all held their breath. The door to their room cracked open just enough to let in a sliver of weak, yellow light from the hallway. Mother stood there, her broken, but beautiful silhouette seeming taller against the light. Her dress was ripped. Its thin fabric was torn open at the shoulder while the hem trailed behind her like a torn flag. There was blood on her arm. A deep gash across her cheek gleamed wetly in the dim light. She smiled even thought one eye was already blue and swollen shut. It was not the kind of smile that reached her eyes, those were too full of pain. It was the kind of smile you wear like a mask, so the ones you love don't see.

"My sweet ones," she whispered in a thick, raw voice. She stepped carefully over the threshold as if the very air hurt her. She slowly knelt beside the mattresses. Her trembling fingers brushed over their faces, smoothed their hair, and finally tucked the blankets tighter under them. She kissed each of them, one by one, her lips shaking against their foreheads. Mother smelled of sorrow and pain. "It's all right now," she said, a lie so big it filled the whole room. "Sleep, my little stars. Sleep."

Athena wanted to reach for her mother, to pull her into their little raft and keep her safe, but no one moved, not even the youngest. They were afraid of making a sound that might bring him in. Mother sat there for a long moment, rocking gently on her knees, her hands folded in her lap like she was praying. Maybe she was looking to God for strength. They all were. Then, with a soft, broken sigh, Mother pushed herself to her feet and limped back toward the door. She glanced back at them, her battered face illuminated by the silver glow behind her. Her eye, the one that could still open, found Athena's. She smiled again, just for her, and then she was gone, swallowed up by the darkness.

Athena lay there listening to the stifled sobs of her brother and sisters while the furious rumbling of her stomach muffled the sound. She stared up at the low ceiling and pictured the sun rising over Lekka, turning the stones to diamonds and the sea to fire. She pictured the blue, endless sky protecting her while she soared high above it all, where fists and boots couldn't reach. She saw a world below her filled by lemon orchards and olive groves. She held that beautiful picture in her mind like a precious coin, clutching it tightly in her heart, and she waited for morning.

Chapter 2: Morning Mist

Morning in Lekka comes early. It slips into the village like a shy cat, brushing against rooftops and stirring the dust in the streets. The first light crept through the crack in our thin ripped curtain, painting a faint stripe across the stone floor. I hadn't slept. None of us had really slept. We lay there on the mattress like washed up driftwood. We lay tangled together, our faces pale, our bodies heavy with the kind of tiredness that no amount of sleep could cure.

I shifted carefully, peeling my sweaty arm away from Katerina's back. She stirred but didn't open her eyes. Little Anna had crawled half onto my chest during the night, her tiny hand curled into the fabric of my dress. Her eyes were swollen from crying and her lashes were clumped together. I turned my head toward the door. It was closed. All was quiet for now. I slowly pushed the threadbare blanket aside and sat up. My head spun a little, but I planted my feet on the cold stone floor and waited for the spinning to pass. The others stayed still, pretending to be asleep.

In our house, if you were the one to wake up first, you carried the morning. You became the protector, the organizer and the shield for the others. You listened at the door. You crept through the kitchen like a mouse, looking for something, anything, to fill the emptiness in our bellies. I stood up and tiptoed to the door, my legs shaking with every step. I pressed my ear against the wooden door and was relieved to hear the heavy, breathless kind of silence I was hoping for.

Mother had taught me when I was small enough to be carried on her hip. She showed me how to move quickly and lightly, so that's what I did. I slipped out into the hallway moving fast, but light. The house smelled sour. The kitchen was empty, no Father and no Mother. For a moment, I let myself breathe. The window above the sink looked out over the village. I stood on my toes to see. Outside, Lekka was waking up. Old Mrs. Theodora was sweeping her front steps with a bundle of twigs. A donkey brayed somewhere up the hill. The warm, sweet smell of bread baking drifted on the breeze. My stomach cramped with hunger. The sky was the color of fresh milk and the sun was not yet strong enough to burn the mist off the hills. It was beautiful. Lekka was always beautiful.

I heard movement and turned. Mother stood in the hallway, her left hand braced against the wall with her face hidden in the shadows. She was still wearing the torn dress from the night before. Her face was blotchy and bruised. Her lip was swollen and her hair matted against her forehead. I could tell that she held herself upright, her chin lifted, her breath slow and even, for me. She smiled a profound smile this time, and spread open her arms to welcome me. I ran into them. Her hug was gentle and careful. She smelled of the faint sweetness of chamomile. For a moment, the world narrowed to Mother resting her cheek against the top of my head. My heart warmed with the sound of her strong, steady heartbeat against my ear.

"We are blessed with a new day," she whispered. I nodded into her shoulder, a tear sliding gently down my cheek. Behind us, the others were waking. I could hear tiny coughs, murmurs and the soft rustle of sheets as my siblings shifted and stretched. Mother pulled away and wiped at my face with the corner of her dress. Her left hand shook, but she steadied it against her thigh. "Go on," she said, her voice stronger now. "Get them up. Wash their faces. I'll find something for breakfast." I didn't ask what. I didn't ask if there was anything to eat. I just nodded again and went back to the mattresses for my sisters and brother. Christina was sitting up now, combing her fingers through her tangled hair. She seemed stiff and sore. Pavlos was trying to soothe Katerina who was crying big, fat tears that slid swiftly down her cheeks. I crouched beside them and touched Aphrodite's hand. "Come on," I said. "Let's go to the well."

Mother had a large, cracked, old basin we used for washing. It was chipped and stained, but it did the jobs we needed it to do. This morning it would catch the cold, clean water we needed to wash our faces. One by one, we helped each other up. We moved slowly, our bodies covered with bruises. Aphrodite picked up Maritza and held her against her hip, even though she was almost too big for that now. Pavlos walked by himself, proud and solemn, like a little general leading an army. In the corner, little Katerina tightly clutched the hem of my dress and we all went out into the brightening morning.

The village square was mostly empty and the stones were still damp with dew. A few chickens scratched in the dust, clucking happily. We passed old Mr. Nikolas who tipped his hat to us without speaking. He knew. Everyone in the village knew, but they were good at pretending. At the well, we filled our big basin and took turns splashing water on our faces. We scrubbed away the stains of dried tears and the sticky residue of fear from our eyes. The cold shocked me awake and made me gasp. Eleni cupped water from the well into her hands and let Christina drink.

Her face was red and swollen, but she smiled, a lopsided, crooked little smile that made my heart ache. When we were done, we sat lined up together, like little soldiers, on the low stone wall while the sun warmed our backs. For a little while, we didn't speak. We just breathed in the gold touched morning.

Across the square, the baker's boy, Anastasios, darted out of the bakery carrying a basket of fresh bread. He glanced our way, then quickly looked down. He seemed almost embarrassed to look at us. He was a kind boy, but too scared to help. I watched him go, the smell of the bread made my stomach growl again. Pavlos must have heard it because he leaned over and bumped his shoulder against mine. I smiled at his teasing gesture. He smiled at me too. Even now, even after everything, we could find these small moments of love and laughter. We would survive because we had to and because all we had was each other.

The bells of Agios Ioannis Prothromos Church rang a clear, sweet sound from the large white structure at the bottom of the hill. The bells filled the air and made the birds rise nervously from the trees. Mother was waiting for us when we came back. There was a large pot of water boiling on the wood burning stove. There were a few ripe peaches and hard biscuits set out on the table. She had tied a scarf around her bruised face. Her hands were busy, moving fast, as if to keep herself from thinking. When she saw us coming, she smiled that bright, beautiful smile that seemed to dare the world to break her. "Come my loves," she said. "Eat. It's a beautiful day." And so we did. We sat around the splintered table, our legs swinging, our mouths full of dry biscuit and fruit while the morning sun poured through the broken shutters. Outside, Lekka bloomed with life. It was a beautiful village of white stones, winding roads and fields of olive trees, stretching across the mountains, looking over the sea. Inside, we were all bruised and battered, but we were together. For now, we needed to be.

Chapter 3: The Lion Returns

The sun was higher now, burning away the last few droplets of dew. The morning smelled of fresh bread, goat's milk, and wild thyme. The narrow streets were turning into glowing rivers of stone in the morning light. We stood along the low stone wall near the village square, sharing the last of the hard biscuits Mother had given us. The crumbs stuck to our fingers and the dry air made our throat scratchy, but none of us complained. We stood here often because Mother asked us to. We watched to see when Father was on his way back so she could make sure everything was to his liking when he arrived. It was good to be outside and to feel the warmth on our faces. We pretended we were just children on any morning, in any village, where fathers came home with smiles instead of frowns.

I was watching a line of ants carrying crumbs across the stones when Eleni stiffened beside me. I followed her gaze down the road that wound from the fields into the heart of Lekka. There he was. Father was making his way back home. Even from far away, you could tell it was him. We saw his distinct, heavy rolling walk, the walk that made him look like he owned the earth he stomped on. He swung his arms widely and carelessly, brushing against market stalls and flower pots without a second thought. He did the same to us.

I swallowed hard waiting for one of us to react. Eleni gasped and then she was off like a shot, running barefoot back toward the house. Her thin legs flashed under her outgrown dress as she raced to warn Mother. The rest of us sat frozen for a moment, staring at his movements. Father was taking his time, talking to people as he passed. Mrs. Stavroula, who sold sweet wine and cheese, gave him a big smile. *"Kalimera Kosta!"* (Good morning Kosta) she called out as if she didn't know where he'd been last night. She tried to make it seem as if she hadn't heard the shouting through the thin village walls when he had erupted at home. Old Mr. Yiannis slapped Father on the back and laughed loudly at something he said. Even the priest, Father Dimitrios gave him a slow nod, but he looked away quickly after.

Everyone knew. Everyone always knew. Father had spent the night at Persefoni's house again, the widow with the heavy bracelets and the deep blue eyes. She lived near the butcher shop, in the house with the blue shutters that never quite closed all the way. The shutters had been open all night. The whole village could see the light burning there. Everyone could hear the laughter. The way Father's voice rose and fell like a bad song echoed throughout the village long after the rest of us had gone silent in the dark. And now, here he was, striding back through town like nothing had happened, like he was the king of Lekka and we were all just peasants bowing at his feet. My stomach twisted. The bread I had eaten turned sour in my mouth. I wanted to spit it out. I wanted to stand up and shout, to tell everyone exactly what he was. He was not the proud lion, not the hardworking farmer, but a man who left bruises on the bodies of the people he was meant to love. But I didn't, because I was fifteen years old and scared, and because even if I shouted, no one would really listen. They would just smile tighter, nod faster and pretend harder, the way they always did.

From the worn stone doorstep of her small whitewashed house, *Yiayia* Athena sat hunched in her cotton shawl, her gnarled hands folded in her lap, her eyes fixed down the hill. Her gaze followed the winding dirt path that led through Lekka's scrub all the way to the edge of the village. She watched with narrowed eyes as the silhouette of her son-in-law staggered into view, his lazy strut and the tip of his cigarette glowing like a demon's eye in the dusk. *Yiayia* knew that he was coming home again, and that meant something would break.

Even though she was old and bent by years of widowhood and wartime scarcity, *Yiayia* Athena's soul remained a sharp edged flame. She had buried a husband, raised five children, and now, even in her last years, she saw with perfect clarity the hell her daughter and grandchildren lived through. She hated it. She hated the way Mother's shoulders folded inward when he approached. She hated the hypocrisy of bruises hidden beneath sleeves, the silences at dinner and the fearful scurrying of our little feet when his boots thudded as he walked.

In Lekka, an old widow had no place to interfere in a man's home, not even when that man was a brute. She could do nothing. She was expected to keep her eyes lowered and her words tucked behind her teeth. Her silence was a tradition that could not be broken.

But *Yiayia* still had something. She had me, her granddaughter Athena. I bore her name, a gift Mother insisted upon despite Father's resistance. *Yiayia* said that from the beginning, she had seen my steady eyes, the bold way I walked, and a silence in me that held fire beneath it. She was proud to say that she saw herself in me. She said that although I was still young, I moved through the world like someone far older, with strength I did not yet understand. *Yiayia* recognized a strength in me and said that it had lived in her once. I was not quite sure what she meant. Now, I noticed her looking at me from her doorstep. I knew she could see the flicker of dread in my eyes when I saw Father in the distance.

Yiayia straightened her back. Our eyes met across the space of the dusty village. *Yiayia* didn't dare to speak, but she tilted her chin just slightly, and raised her brows in that silent, wordless language only women in pain can speak. Her mouth didn't move, but her expression said everything, *Don't worry my girl. You are stronger than he is. Stronger than all of this. You will make things right. One day, you will rise. For all of us.* I looked at her and just barely nodded. I bent my head just enough so that *Yiayia* could see my determination. I could see the hope in her eyes. Her satisfied smirk showed me what she was thinking. *Her granddaughter was watching and learning. I would grow up and carry the name well. I would carry them all.*

Father reached the square. I could see the dark stains on his shirt, the loose buckle of his belt and the redness in his face. He smelled of stale tobacco. His eyes were sharp like a crow's flicking over us, counting, one, two, three, four... Where was Eleni? Where was Mother? Where were the rest of us? He frowned in confusion. For a second, I thought he would stomp toward to the house. I pictured him chasing Eleni while roaring like a wounded beast. He twitched and then seemed to remember he was still in the village square while still on display. He smiled a great, toothy grin that showed his bright white teeth. That smile made my skin crawl. He opened his arms wide, as if to embrace us all. "My little lambs!" he boomed. "What a beautiful day God has given us!"

The villagers looked, their faces tight and strained, but they still smiled back at him. Mr. Nikolas pretended to adjust his hat. Mrs. Theodora continued sweeping invisible dust from her doorstep. No one really looked too closely. They never did. Father continued toward us. Pavlos, always quick to please and eager to calm him, jumped down from the wall and ran to him. Father laughed and swung him up onto his hip with a grunt of effort. "Ah, my strong boy!" he said. "My lion cub!" He ruffled Pavlos' hair roughly, making him wince, but Pavlos just smiled harder. The rest of us bowed our heads and slid down from the wall, our feet scuffing the dirt. I stayed where I was. I did not move. I did not smile. Father's eyes found mine. They narrowed. "Athena," he said, trying to sound sweet. "No good morning kiss for your *Baba*?"

I felt the heat rise in my cheeks while I stared at him. I pressed my lips together so hard, they hurt. I could feel the others around me shifting anxiously, begging me silently, *Please, Athena. Please don't make him angry,* but today I could not. I didn't move, nor did I speak to him. I bowed my head just enough to be respectful, then I glanced back at *Yiayia*. She nodded. Father made a low, displeased sound deep in his throat. It sounded like a dog warning just before it bites. His hand twitched at his side, but he didn't strike me. Instead, he let out a sharp, ugly laugh sound that made the hair on my arms stand up. He set Pavlos down roughly and clapped his hands. "Come now," he said. "Let's go home. Your mother must have something warm waiting for us." I looked at *Yiayia* again. Her disgust filled expression said it all, *Another hypocrisy, another one of his lies.*

We all followed behind him, small and silent, like broken kites behind a storm. I saw the way the villagers looked at us as we passed. Their glances showed pity tangled with fear. They knew and they did nothing. Somehow, that made it all worse. Our bare feet dragged slowly and heavily through the dust as we walked back to the house. Pavlos clutched my hand so tight that his fingers hurt mine, but I didn't let go. As Father walked in front of us whistling a tuneless song, my stomach flipped over itself like a fish caught in a net. I squeezed Pavlos' hand just as strongly and steadily as he squeezed mine. Father seemed like he didn't have a care in the world. He kicked a stone down the path and sent it bouncing off a crumbling wall. He laughed when Christina flinched. We all looked, but no one said a word. The sun beat down on our heads, warm and golden, but inside us, there was only cold.

Eleni, fast as she was, must have warned Mother that he was coming, so the door was already open when we reached the house. Mother had done what she always did. She made everything look as good as she could, trying to prevent the worst. Inside, the small windows were letting in only narrow streams of light and a bit of thick, hot air. The battered table had been wiped clean with a wet rag. A plate of olives sat in the center alongside a small loaf of bread and a few pieces of thin, crumbling, goat cheese. It wasn't much. It never was, but Mother had made it look like a feast. She stood near the wood stove wearing a fresh scarf tied tightly around her bruised face. She seemed calm even though we knew how she felt. Her torn dress was mended clumsily with uneven stitches. When Father walked in, she smiled a bright, sharp smile that didn't reach her swollen eyes. "Welcome home, Kosta," she said in a sweet, clear voice. Father grunted. He stomped across the room, letting his boots clatter hard against the stone floor, and threw himself into the chair at the head of the table.

We hurried to our places, like mice scattering from a broom. Mother moved quickly. She poured water into chipped, clay cups, setting them in front of each of us with careful hands. "Eat," Father barked. "Don't just sit there like beggars." We obeyed, tearing small pieces of bread and cheese, eating slowly and carefully with our heads down. Pavlos sat beside Father, puffing out his little chest like a soldier. He grinned a wide smile, eating quickly, trying to make Father proud. He always tried to be noticed for the right reasons. That was his way of protecting us. Father reached out and clapped Pavlos' back, nearly knocking him into the table. "That's my boy," he said. "Strong and brave, just like Father."

Those words made my skin crawl. Across from me, Christina's hands trembled as she brought the cup to her lips. She spilled a little on her dress but quickly wiped it away before Father could notice. Little Anna gnawed on a piece of bread while her teeth chattered. Only Katerina didn't eat. She sat in my lap, her face buried against my chest, breathing deeply. I tore a bit of bread free and tried to coax it into her mouth, but she turned her head away. Father noticed. His eyes sharpened. "What's wrong with her?" he said, his voice dangerously low. "Nothing," I said quickly. "She's just tired." Father stared at me for a long moment. The room felt like it was holding its breath, as we were.

Father could not be fooled. He knew everything we did and heard everything we said. He was everywhere. Even when he wasn't in the room, his presence pressed down on the house like a heavy blanket in summer heat. Every movement was accounted for. Every word we said was measured. He believed order was the spine of a good home, and he was the backbone that held it upright. Nothing escaped his eye, not the way the bread was sliced, nor how long we lingered at the market, and certainly not the cut of a hem.

Father insisted on overseeing every detail, even the way we dressed for a swim, not that we were permitted to swim often. He forbade us from going to the sea in Karlovassi unless he was present, and he rarely was. The beach, he said, was a place of temptation and a theater of sins. If we ever went swimming, it was under strict orders, chaperoned by Mother or an older male cousin. We were made to wear long, heavy cotton dresses that stuck to our legs when wet, weighing us down like a punishment. We weren't allowed to splash or laugh too loudly. "You are not peasants," he'd scold. "You are respectable girls from Lekka. Carry yourselves as such." Before every rare outing, he'd inspect our clothes himself, dragging his fingers along the seams, tugging at sleeves to check the width, making sure the coverage was suffice. Any signs of styles that flirted with modern designs were swiftly reprimanded and quickly corrected. On one such morning, as the heat began to settle in the stones of the yard, Father summoned Aphrodite while he was sipping his coffee.

"Remember," he said, without looking up from his cup, "when sewing your sisters' dresses this afternoon, do not forget what I told you." Aphrodite stood straight, hands behind her back and nodded. "You will measure the length from the knees down. Start at the knee, and the length should be one forearm's length below the knee, for all the girls' dresses." He raised his eyes, then fixed them on her with the sharp stare that cut deeper than his words. "Do not make them short like last time, Aphrodite! Do you understand?"

"Yes, Father," she said quietly while lowering her eyes.

He nodded once, seeming satisfied. Then he turned his attention to the window. He watched the village below for a few seconds as if daring it to disobey him. Even the tailor in Karlovassi had learned to keep his distance from our family. Father accused him of shortening a hem on purpose, to shame the girls. The man had nervously laughed, thinking it was a joke, until Father stopped him mid laugh and said, "I don't joke about my daughters." That was before Aphrodite learned how to sew our clothes for us. Now he had complete control of everything we wore. With Father, the rules were never just rules. They were walls, high ones. We learned early on that there was no climbing over Father's walls.

With a grunt, Father shoved his chair back from the table and stood. The legs scraped hard against the stone. "I'm going to the fields," he said. "The sun won't wait for lazy men." He grabbed his hat off the hook by the door and shoved it onto his head. At the door, he turned back once, his eyes sweeping over us. I met his gaze for a heartbeat and something inside me burned so hot, I began to sweat. I didn't look away. Father's lip curled at my defiance, but he said nothing to me. Then, he was gone, the door slamming behind him. The cups rattled on the table, yet the silence he left behind was almost eerie. For a moment, no one moved. Then Mother exhaled a long, shuddering breath and dropped into the nearest chair.

I eased Katerina off my lap and went to Mother. I didn't say anything, I just placed my hand on her arm as lightly and carefully as I could. She turned her head toward me. Her eyes were red and raw and her scarf slipped down slightly, revealing the ugly bruise blooming along her forehead. She smiled at me. I think she felt that she had to, for us. She always did everything for us. She cupped my cheek in her palm. Her skin was rough but warm. "My brave girl," she whispered. I pressed my face into her hand and closed my eyes. I made a promise then, not with words, but with the fierce thudding of my heart. *I will protect you. I will protect them. I will never become like him. No matter what. No matter how long it takes. I promise!*

Chapter 4: The Promise

Our bruises were painted gold by the morning light seeping sightly through the shutters. Outside, Lekka sang with the sounds of life, roosters crowing, goats bleating and children laughing in the distance. Inside, we held onto each other. Inside, we survived and we dreamed because for now, dreams were all we had.

The afternoon pressed down like a giant hand. The air inside the house grew thicker, smelling of dust, sweat, and the faint sourness of mold. The little ones curled up on the mattresses, their bodies limp with exhaustion. No one dared speak too loudly. No one dared drop a plate or knock over a stool. The walls were thin and seemed to echo every noise straight into the fields where Father worked, if he wasn't at her house again. Even from Pesefoni's house, he could hear, and if he heard something he didn't like, we knew what he would do.

Eleni's hands were chapped from scrubbing the floor, but she didn't stop. Christina washed the worn clothes in the cracked basin by the door, her arms aching from the cold water and the rough stone scrubbing board. By mid afternoon, the chores were done, or rather, done enough to avoid trouble. The house had gone silent again, except for the soft breathing of sleeping children. Maritza and I slipped outside carefully, the door creaking just a little as it swung shut behind us. We knew what we had to do. We were off to work. I was to turn the soil and prepare the land near the olive grove to get it ready for planting. Maritza was to mind the sheep at the top of the mountain.

The world outside was blinding with light. The white stones of the path dazzled my eyes, and the sky was an endless, roaring blue. We ran past the wall where the well stood, past the huddled houses and past the dusty olive press, our feet slapping the warm earth while the calluses on our soles drank in the heat. Maritza and I split up at the bend near the bakery. She ran towards the sound of the sheep at the top of the mountain and I headed to the fields. I didn't stop until I reached the olive groves. The trees twisted like dancers in the sun and their leaves seemed to be whispering secrets to each other. The ground was dry and cracked, but between the roots of the oldest trees, small wildflowers bloomed to show tiny flashes of white and purple against the brown earth.

I dropped to my knees in the grass and pressed my forehead against the rough bark of one of the trees. Some said that the olive trees were ancient and that they had been here longer than any of us, even longer than Lekka itself. I liked to think they remembered everything, every laughter and every cry and somehow, with the weight of all these memories, they stayed standing. I wanted to be like those trees. I wanted to be tall, big and strong like them. I lay back in the dirt looking up through the silver green leaves at the blinding blue beyond with my rusted shovel in hand. The earth was warm under me and the sky above me told stories of bright futures. The ache in my chest loosened while I gazed at the sky. I let my mind drift again. I imagined a different life. I imagined a house made of bright white stone and white shutters that never slammed shut in anger. I imagined a mother who sang while she cooked and a father who lifted us onto his shoulders, laughing, not shouting. I imagined my brother and sisters running free in the fields, our bellies full, our knees scraped from climbing trees instead of kneeling on hard floors. In my dreams, I was strong, fast and ferocious. In my dreams, no one told me to keep my head down and in my dreams, I had wings.

I heard footsteps crunching over dry grass and sat up quickly, my heart pounding. It was Pavlos. I breathed a sigh of relief. Breathing hard, he flopped down beside me and smiled a crooked grin. "Found you," he said, poking me with a stick. I rolled my eyes and swatted him away. "You're loud as a goat," I said. He laughed, a swift, howling sound, and lay back with his arms spread wide like he wanted to soak up all the sun in the world. For a few minutes, we just lay there, side by side, saying nothing. The loud buzzing sound of cicadas filled our ears and calmed my soul. We could see a hawk circling lazily overhead. Finally, Pavlos turned his head towards me. "Do you think it'll ever change?" he asked, his voice almost too quiet to hear.

I swallowed hard and thought about lying. I wanted to say yes, of course it will, everything will be better someday, but he deserved more than lies. He deserved the truth. "I don't know," I said.

He stared up at the sky. After a while, he said, "When I'm big, I'll change it." I looked at his thin arms and noticed the purple shadow fading on his cheek, above the collar of his patched shirt. He was small and powerless. We all were, for now.

"Me too," I said, and I meant it. We stayed there until the sun lay lower and its light turned honey and gold. I knew we had to go back before Father returned. We knew he was not in the fields where he said he would be, and we knew where he was. Persefoni's house was where he wanted to be. It was there that he laughed, that he smiled, and that he loved to be. For just a little while longer, Pavlos and I let the olive trees shelter us. We let the wildflowers brush our skin while we let ourselves dream, because dreams made everything bearable. I didn't work the soil that afternoon. I did not want to. I wanted to dream alongside my brother. If I dreamed hard enough, I thought perhaps I could magically force my dreams to come true. After a few more minutes under the sinking sun, Pavlos and I began our return home from the fields.

The sun was a bleeding orange on the horizon by that time. The light stretched shadows across the dirt paths making everything look strange and twisted. The stones, the trees, even the shapes of the houses leaned and swayed as if the village itself was holding its breath. Pavlos kicked at the dust as we walked. His hands were jammed into his pockets. I could feel the weight pulling him down, as it did me, but neither of us said a word. Words wouldn't stop what was waiting for us. Nothing could. We passed by Mrs. Stavroula's house, where the sweet, thick smell of baking clung to the air. I thought of her warm kitchen, the heavy, braided breads she made for her sons and how her laughter used to spill out of the windows in the evenings. And I thought of our house, filled with children, yet silent.

As we approached the house, heavy tension crept into our bones. I planned silently as we got to the house. I pictured Father's presence already filling the house like smoke. We turned the last corner, and there it was, our battered little home, crouched low to the ground, the shutters pulled closed like the eyes of a wounded animal. The door stood ajar, which was a very bad sign. Pavlos slowed, then stopped altogether, his face pale under the dirt smudges. I touched his arm lightly. "We have to go in," I whispered. He nodded, but he didn't move, and for a long moment, neither did I. Then, forcing myself, I pushed the door open wider.

Inside, the air was heavy with a sharp smell beneath the air that reminded me of old, rotting anger. Father was already home. He sat at the table, his shoulders hunched, his head low between his fists. A half empty bottle stood by his elbow. A line of olives spilled across the plate, their sharp brine spilling over the dish, soaking into the wooden table. Mother was near the stove. Her body was small and stiff. One of her hands pressed against her ribs above her apron. The other hand, shaking with the weight it carried, held a jug of water. The little ones huddled on the mattress. Their faces were tight with fear. Aphrodite held Katerina close, wrapping her arms around her like a metal shield. Tiny Anna whimpered quietly into her own shoulder, the sound barely more than a breath.

Father didn't look up when we entered. My feet made a squeaking sound as they slid along the cement floor. Pavlos stayed rooted just behind me. I wanted to turn and shove him back out the door. I wanted to send him away, anywhere but here, but it was too late.

Father lifted his head. His eyes wild and bloodshot, pinned us in place. "Where were you?" he said, his voice hoarse and stern.

The bottle wobbled as he tried to push himself to his feet. I opened my mouth, trying to find a soft harmless lie, but my tongue stuck to the roof of my mouth. Pavlos jumped in to speak first. "Gathering kindling," he said quickly and clearly.

Father stared at him for a long, horrible moment. Then, grimacing disgust covered his face. He tried to stand, but couldn't. He slapped the table with his left hand and dropped back into his chair. "Useless," he muttered. "Good for nothing children." Mother moved carefully. She set down a chipped plate with a few boiled potatoes onto the table in front of Father. She didn't look him in the eye, and she didn't speak. She didn't have to. Her actions spoke fear.

Father ate noisily, tearing into the food like a wild animal while oil ran down his chin. We all stood frozen, waiting and praying. We prayed that today would not be like yesterday, or the yesterday before that. The only sounds we could hear were the scrape of his fork and the tiny, uncontrollable whimpers from the mattress where Eleni and Christina trembled together. Father's ear twitched toward the sound. I gasped as I saw the slow turn of his head and the narrowing of his eyes. I felt my heart seize for a moment, but I moved fast, before he could. I crossed the room in two quick strides and dropped onto the mattress between the little ones. I threw my arms around them and rocked them gently murmuring soft, nonsense words into their hair, trying to muffle their cries. "Shh, shh, little birds," I whispered. "Safe, safe, shh." Father watched me for a moment, then snorted and turned back to his plate in disgust. The danger barely passed, but the fear didn't. It stayed, thick and sour, crawling under our skin and into our bones. I sat there on the mattress cradling my siblings, my muscles locked tight with tension and for the first time, I realized something with a sharp clarity that made my stomach ache, *This would not end unless I ended it. We couldn't just survive. We had to escape. Someday, somehow, we had to get out. All of us, or none of us would.*

That night, after Father stumbled off to bed and the bottle lay empty on the floor, Mother came to check on us. She knelt beside the mattress, gathering us close with quivering hands. She had removed the scarf from her head. The bruises stood out stark and purple in the moonlight, painting her face like a map, a map of all the places she had been hurt. But her voice was soft, almost singing. "My sweet babies," she whispered. "My doves. My strong ones." She kissed each forehead, one by one, her breath hitching slightly as she bent over Pavlos who whimpered in his sleep.

When she reached me, she paused. Her fingers lingered against my cheek tracing the faint outline of an old scar, a gift from Father's belt buckle two summers ago. I caught her hand in mine and I squeezed hard. She smiled. Then, a real smile emerged. Although her smile was cracked and battered, it sparkled of hope. In that moment, I made a second, fiercer promise, *We will leave. We will live. I don't care what it costs. Dreams might be enough for a while, but not forever. Forever needed a plan, and I would make one.*

Chapter 5, Brave and Strong

Morning came hard. The thin mattress offered little comfort and my neck ached from sleeping curled around the little ones. But the sun still rose, and so did we. There was no time for stretching or yawning, only the slap of cold water on our faces, the hurried braiding of hair and the pulling on of patched clothes, still damp from last night's washing. Mother moved stiffly around the kitchen, her bruises stark against her pale skin. She barely spoke. Neither did we. The air inside the house was filled with things unsaid. Father had left before sunrise, stomping off to the fields with a muttered curse about "lazy children" and "thankless women." We knew the drill, finish the chores, keep the little ones quiet, pray he came back tired enough not to raise his hand again.

I carried little Anna on my hip as we fed the goats, three scrawny, mean tempered creatures who butted at our legs and nipped at our fingers. Christina and Eleni gathered eggs from the tiny hen house, tucking them carefully into their aprons. Pavlos hauled water from the well, his thin arms straining with every heavy bucket. As I worked, my eyes stayed sharp. I noticed things now. Small things. Important things, like how Mrs. Stavroula sometimes slipped Mother a cloth bundle of bread and dried figs when no one was looking. Or how old man Dimos, crouched forward with arthritis, would turn his face away when Father staggered past. He did not avoid Father out of cowardice, but because he knew, and he hated what he saw. I noticed which paths stayed hidden under the olive trees and which wells lay half forgotten behind crumbling walls. I noticed that if you climbed high enough up the goat trail, you could see straight across the island, all the way to the glittering sea. Freedom shimmered there, just beyond the hills. I carried these things inside me like seeds, tucked snugly into the earth in the fields. My thoughts were growing, and patiently waiting.

At the market that afternoon, Mother sent Aphrodite and me to trade a bundle of herbs for a bit of flour and oil. The square in Lekka buzzed with life. We heard women bartering loudly over heads of cabbage, old men playing dice in the shade and children chasing each other through the dust. In the horizon, the sea shimmered with hope. The mountainside glared with prosperity. It should have been a beautiful, bustling scene, but Aphrodite and I moved through it like ghosts, eyes flicking from face to face, cataloging them all. Who could be trusted? Who looked away? Who smiled too easily at Father's jokes? I tucked the knowledge away carefully as I planned our escape, our freedom and peace.

At the flour stall, I handed over the herbs and watched as Mr. Lefteris weighed them on rusty scales. He gave us a little extra, slipping it into the sack with a quick glance around, like he didn't want anyone to see. Perhaps it was pity, or possibly guilt? I didn't care. I nodded my thanks and moved on. Beside the well, Mrs. Stavroula caught my arm gently. "How's your mother, child?" she asked in a low voice, her thick fingers squeezing mine. "She's strong," I said, because it was true. Mrs. Stavroula's mouth tightened, and she said no more. Instead, she pressed something into my hand. It was a crumpled piece of cloth. Inside were two boiled eggs and a small handful of almonds. "For the little ones." she muttered. I tucked the bundle into my apron pocket without a word. I could not refuse and I knew better than to cry. We finished our errands quickly, keeping our heads down then hurried back home before the sun dipped too low. Father hated latecomers.

At the house, we found Pavlos and Christina sitting on the stoop, their faces smudged and tired. Mother sat inside, rocking little Anna against her chest, her lips moving silently in prayer. The light through the cracked shutters painted her in gold dust, a symbol and statue of survival. As I stood there, the sack of flour cutting into my arms, I knew the day was coming when I would save them. I would save us all. I was Athena, named for the goddess of wisdom and war. *Yiayia* Athena said that even the smallest seed can crack the hardest stone, if it is patient enough. I just had to wait, watch, plan and grow.

At night, when the little ones finally stilled and Father's snores shook the broken rafters overhead, I lay awake, my eyes wide open to the blackness. The house was thick with heat and the smell of unwashed bodies. Our shared mattresses sagged under the weight of us all like a narrow, worn island in a sea of fear. I listened to the whimpering of the youngest and the soft grinding of Pavlos' teeth while they slept. I heard the rumbling growl of empty stomachs that never seemed to stop. The faint creaking of shutters in the midnight breeze could be heard, along with the far off barking of a stray dog. Above it all, in the distant mountains, the occasional sharp crack of rifle fire echoed, faint, but there. It was a reminder. Greece was breaking apart at the seams. The war with the Germans had ended, but peace had not come. Now brother fought brother, village fought village. Royalists loyal to the King clashed with rebels who dreamed of a different Greece, a free Greece, a Greece for the poor, hungry and beaten down. A Greece for people like me.

The grownups whispered about it when they thought we weren't listening. They quietly spoke about the men, and some women, who had fled to the mountains, living like wolves, hidden in caves and forests, fighting back against the government and the rich landowners who had bled them dry for generations. They called the rebels anarchists, communists and traitors. Mother only ever called them "our last hope" when she thought we couldn't hear. Eleni and I knew better than to ask questions out loud, but we knew. We heard the village boys talking in low, urgent voices when they thought no one was near. We saw the secret signs scratched into the stones near the well, a star, a sickle and a clenched fist. We saw the way Mrs. Stavroula wrapped a loaf of bread in cloth and slipped it to a young man with a rifle slung across his back.

We all knew, and I wanted in. It started with small things when Father was with Persefoni. He would never allow us to wander in the night. So when he wasn't there, we'd run to the orchards to quietly collect a few peaches. Sometimes, Mr. Lefteris would leave out a loaf of bread, knowing that we would deliver it to the soldiers. Eleni and I climbed the back trails under the cover of darkness, breathing hard, hearts pounding while stones dug into our bare feet. The first time Eleni and I went there, we were scared and almost turned back, but we didn't. Once we had given the food to the soldiers, Eleni grabbed my hand tight and whispered, "We can't stay here forever, Athena." I didn't agree with her. We delivered the food to a man named Nikos, a big, broad shouldered farmer who had once been our neighbor. He didn't smile when he took the bundle from us, but his rough hand squeezed my shoulder gently before he melted back into the shadows. After that, it became a rhythm. Every few nights, a small package, a whispered greeting, a skittering dash up the hidden goat paths, and sometimes, Panayiotis was there, big, brave and handsome Panayiotis.

Panayiotis was older, possibly older than eighteen. His wild blond curls and dark eyes burned like coals when he looked at me. He wore an army jacket, two sizes too big and carried a battered rifle slung over his back like a second spine. When he spoke, which was not often, it was like the rocks themselves had cracked open and found a strong, steady voice. He was just the man that could protect me, protect us from Father, especially since he was Persefoni's brother. Father would respect him. Besides, Panayiotis was a strong, brave man, and he was a fighter. Father would surely respect him.

The first time I met Panayiotis, the basket I was carrying slid from my hands. His fingers brushed mine as he caught it easily in one hand. Then he smiled, not a mocking smile like the boys in the village who sneered and jostled each other and pointed to our feet. No, Panayiotis' smile was different. Something that said, *I see you. Not just the dirt, the bare feet and the ragged dress. I see you and the fire burning inside you.* After that day, I looked for him whenever we climbed the trails. I carried extra peaches, just in case he was there. I memorized the shape of his shadow against the rocks. I dreamed of him when the nights were long and the mattress too crowded for me to be able to sleep. I knew better than to think of love. There was no space for love in my life, but I still carried him inside me like blood, warm and bright, something that no one could take away. And somewhere along the way, a plan began to form. It was not just a child's desperate hope anymore, it was a real plan, a clear and precise plan.

Chapter 6: The Plan

I went through every step in my mind, mentally numbering each step. *1. Wait for a night when Father was snoring loud enough not to notice. 2. Pack only what I could carry, a little food, a little water, the sewing needles, a small knife. 3. Take the goat trail past the old mill, where the rocks split into a narrow ravine. 4. Leave the village behind, climb high into the mountains where the fighters lived like smoke and shadows. 5. I would take Pavlos and Eleni with me.* Mother would have to decide for the little ones. I couldn't carry them all, and it broke my heart in two. *If I tried to save everyone, I might save no one*, I thought to myself. *6. Once in the mountains, I would join the fighters. Not just as a helper, but as one of them.* I could be a fighter with a voice and a blade, like Panayiotis. I could cook. I could mend clothes, but more than anything, I could fight. I would fight for a new Greece, and fight for a life where the world wasn't measured by bruises, broken bones and hunger gnawing at your ribs. I could fight for my siblings to have a childhood, and fight for all of us to finally be able to breathe. The plan was dangerous. It was almost madness, but it was real. It was possible, and that made it everything I could think of.

That night, lying on the mattress with Eleni's hand curled in mine, the hot air pressed down on us like a curse. I closed my eyes and repeated the steps over and over in my mind: *Wait, pack, run, climb, fight, live and finally breath relief.* For the first time since I started planning, the fear didn't crush me. It sharpened and honed me. I wasn't just a little girl lying in the dark, praying for miracles anymore. I was Athena, daughter of storms, daughter of wisdom, daughter of war, and soon, very soon, daughter of freedom.

The final days before the escape blurred together like a half remembered dream. Each morning, I woke with a tight knot in my stomach. Every night, I fell asleep rehearsing the steps like a prayer. *Wait, pack, run, climb, fight and live.* The goat trail we would take wound up behind the olive grove where the ground cracked into narrow gullies hidden by tall dry grass. Past the stone wall that leaned sideways sat a shack, half collapsed from last winter's rains. Across the dry creek that only ran water in the spring, the picturesque view of endless, wild and sharp mountains resembled broken teeth against the sky. The higher trails twisted through dense thickets of cypress and pine. The ground was littered with needles and crumbling bark. The air up there smelled different, sharper, cleaner, full of wild thyme, oregano and salt blown in from the sea. I could see it in my mind like a painted map. I pictured the bend in the trail where the red rock jutted out like a crooked finger, the hollow tree trunk where Nikos had told us to hide if the army patrols came, and the secret spring where cold, clear water bubbled up from the roots of an ancient olive tree. Freedom lived up there, waiting and calling for me.

On the day of the escape, everything felt sharp and bright. The sun blazed down like lightning, baking the dust until it cracked and curled. The cicadas screamed from the earth tonight. The sound felt like a wild, endless drone that set my teeth on edge. Pavlos kept fidgeting, his skinny hands twisting the hem of his shirt. Eleni was quieter than usual, her eyes darting toward the door every few minutes. We were ready. *"Tonight. Finally, tonight,"* I whispered under my breath. The little bundle I had packed waited under the hearthstone. It huddled a handful of olives, a heel of bread, a sewing needle, a small but sharp knife, and a tiny portrait of Mother as a girl, smiling shyly and beautifully in the sunlight. This was for luck, for memory and something to fight for. I was near the goat trail when I saw Marika. My heart thumped so loudly it drowned out the sounds of the island.

Marika was only a little older than me, a neighbor girl with quick eyes and a mouth too loose for secrets. She stood by the fence near the trail, pretending to pluck at weeds, her gaze flickering toward us. She was watching and listening. I froze with a sick, heavy feeling dropping into my gut.

Later that afternoon, Mother's voice called sharp across the yard. "Athena! Come here." Mother's face was tight, the lines around her mouth white with strain. Inside the house, Aunt Venetia was sitting stiffly at the table. She wore a knitted shawl wrapped around her narrow shoulders even though the heat made the walls sweat. My heart shriveled. I knew something was wrong. Mother sat me down hard on the bench, her hands fluttering like trapped birds. "You're planning something," she said. It was not a question, it was a statement. My mouth opened and instantly slammed shut. I didn't know what to say because I knew that Mother already knew.

Aunt Venetia leaned forward, her voice urgent and low. "You think you're running to freedom little one, but you're running into war. You don't know what it's like up there. There is hunger, cold, guns and great danger!" She gripped my wrist hard. "You'll die on those mountains Athena."

"I won't," I said fiercely, yanking my arm free.

Mother's face crumpled like thin paper folding in on itself while blatant fear enveloped her face. She took a shaky breath and at that moment, I knew that I could not do this to her. Mother's face never looked that way, even when Father was about to erupt. "Marika heard you and Eleni talking near the well. She ran straight to me." Mother's voice trembled with fear. "And if Father finds out?" The air went out of the room.

I knew what she meant without her saying it. If Father found out I was planning to leave, to join the communists, to shame his name and steal his 'pride and joy' Pavlos away, the beatings would be the least of it. He could kill me, kill Mother, kill us all, maybe not all at once, but slowly, surely, and piece by piece. Terror clawed at my throat. Mother urgently grabbed both my hands, and held them tight. "I called your uncle Petros in Athens," she said.

My head snapped up. "Athens?"

"Yes." Aunt Venetia nodded grimly. "He has connections. He can get you work. In a laundry, maybe in his *taverna*, but somewhere safe. Anywhere is safer than those God forbidden mountains."

"Safe," Mother repeated, tears filling her eyes. "You will be free, not fighting, not here with us, but you will be safe."

"You're leaving the day after tomorrow," Aunt Venetia blurted. "Before he knows and before anyone else finds out." My heart slammed against my ribs so hard it hurt. Tomorrow? Gone? Everything I had dreamed of, the mountains, the trail, the fighters, Panayiotis, all slipping away like smoke between my fingers. I sat there, numb, as Mother and Aunt Venetia whispered about ferry schedules and forged papers and how to sneak me onto the ferry boat without Father catching scent. I barely heard them. I was already drifting, floating, adrift, between the old life and the one being thrust upon me. Not the life I chose, but possibly the life I needed to survive. Surely, it was the life that Mother, my sisters and my brother needed to survive from Father's fury.

That night, lying on the mattress between my sleeping siblings, I listened to the familiar sounds of our cramped, broken world, the whimpering, the grinding of teeth, the endless growling of empty bellies, but above it all, I heard something else, the slow, steady roar of change. It was coming like a storm rolling over the mountains. Whether I ran to meet it, or was carried away against my will, I would not drown. I would not break. I was Athena, daughter of storms, daughter of wisdom, daughter of war, and somehow, some way, I would find my way. I just didn't know which way was mine anymore.

Chapter 7: Curse to the First Journey

It happened faster than any of us could stop it. Marika might have gone to Mother first, but she didn't stop there. Loose tongues in small villages are like matches in dry grass. One word to her cousin, another to the baker's wife, a passing whisper to old Manolis at the *kafeneio* (coffee shop) and by the next morning, the whole village knew, and by mid morning, Father knew.

I was in the garden behind the house, digging for onions, when the shouting started. His voice tore through the still air like a knife. "Athena!" I froze, my heart knocking against my ribs. The onions slipped from my fingers. Footsteps pounded toward me. Dust boiled up under his heavy boots and before I could run, before I could even stand, Father's hand closed around the back of my neck like an iron trap. "You think you're clever, little whore?" he hissed into my ear, his breath sour with raki and rage. He dragged me into the road, past the water well, past Mother who was screaming after us and past the neighbors peeking from behind their curtains. I struggled, but he was stronger. He always was. He pushed me down the hill to the town square. It was blistering hot and the stone beneath my bare feet burned like coals. Father shoved me forward so hard I stumbled to my knees. He took hold of my long, black, curl filled hair. He tugged, putting my head to the ground. Several townspeople stood nearby, pretending not to look, but they were looking all the same. Their faces pinched with curiosity, disgust, or fear, but nobody said a word.

With my hair still in his iron grip, he leaned forward towards my feet and spat. "A daughter who betrays her blood!" he roared. "A daughter who leaves her home! A daughter who takes her siblings into the night, a night filled with guns and danger! *"Ἀνάθεμα σε Athena!"* (Curse on you, Athena) "May shame, sweat and the swirling of dust swallow your every step!" His voice echoed off the stone walls, bouncing from shuttered window to shuttered window. "A girl who runs from her family is no daughter of mine," he bellowed, throwing his arms wide so that everyone could see. "She spits on the graves of her ancestors! She spits on me!" He spat again, closer this time, the wet sound hitting the stones with a sickening slap. I lay there, trembling. My skin burned under the gaze of the village. Shame wrapped around me like a suffocating shroud. Hot tears blurred my vision, but I blinked them back furiously. I would not cry for him. Not here, not ever. Father loomed over me, his shadow a jagged thing stretched across the dust. "May your womb dry up like old figs," he said, voice low and hateful. Then he turned his back to me and walked away, leaving me lying in the swirling of dust from his path, alone and ridiculed.

Mother came to me almost instantly, her breath hitching in her chest. She dropped to her knees beside me, gathering me into her arms, rocking me like a baby. "I'm sorry, Athena *mou*," she whispered, over and over again. "I'm sorry. I'm sorry. I'm sorry." But it wasn't her fault. It had never been her fault.

That night, as the house grew dark and the children curled together like kittens for comfort, I lay awake. I watched them, little hands curled into fists, little mouths open in silent, shuddering dreams. My heart broke into a thousand sharp pieces. I couldn't take them all with me, but I could get out. I could find a way to bring them with me, but not now. I would come back stronger, stronger than fear, poverty and stronger than Father. I pressed my hand against Pavlos' sleeping back. I felt the steady rise and fall of his breath, and made a silent promise: *"I will come back for you."* I would come back for all of them. Eleni, so fierce and brave. Christina, who still cried for Mama's lullabies at night. Little Anna, who barely knew a world beyond these walls. For Mother, who bore the weight of the world on her bruised shoulders and still managed to sing sometimes. I would not abandon them forever. I would not be swallowed by the city, or broken by loneliness. I would build something, a new life, a new way, a way big enough to bring them all into the light. I pressed my palm against my thigh, feeling the reassuring weight through the thin cotton of my dress. Tomorrow, the boat. Tomorrow, Athens. Tomorrow, is the first step in the longest journey of my life.

The night was ink black when Mother shook me awake. "Athena," she whispered urgently, her hands gently shaking my shoulders. "Now." The house was silent except for the soft, ragged breathing of my brother and sisters curled like kittens on the worn mattresses. I dressed quickly, fumbling in the dark. My shoes were old and too small for my feet. My dress, a lovely pink, was patched a dozen times over. Mother pressed a small cloth bundle into my hands. It held some dried figs, a crust of bread, and a handkerchief wrapped around three, gold colored coins. She kissed my forehead once and whimpered. "No matter what happens, don't look back Athena," she said. "Don't run. Walk. Quiet like a cat." I nodded, swallowing the lump that had risen into my throat.

Outside, the crickets sang their endless night song. The moon hung low and heavy like a silver coin dropping into the black velvet sky. Aunt Venetia was waiting by the olive tree, her hair wrapped in her dark handkerchief. She glanced nervously toward the road. We moved quickly, keeping to the shadows. The village slept, or pretended to. The *kafeneio* (coffee shop) doors were shuttered. The smell of burnt wood and goat lingered in the air. The sea whispered somewhere beyond the hills. My feet made almost no sound on the dust. Each step felt like walking across the end of a blade. At the edge of the village, where the dirt road turned rocky and the low stone walls crumbled into the fields, I saw them. The soldiers stood there, weapons in hand. There were three of them, rifles slung casually over their shoulders. They were laughing low and mean in the night. They were waiting, patrolling the dock. My heart seized. I grabbed Mother's hand tightly, and for a moment, just a moment, I wanted to scream, to run back to the safety of our little house, to hide under the saggy mattresses with my brother and sisters and pretend this night had never come. Then I saw Father's face in my mind, twisted with rage while spitting blasphemous words into the dust. I saw the bruises blooming like dark flowers on Mother's arms. I saw my brother and sisters, the stagnant future that waited for them if I went back, or if I failed to get them out. *No! I would not go back. And I would not fail!*

We waited in the shadows of the last wall, hearts pounding in our chests like trapped eagles. The soldiers passed, laughing about something, their boots striking the stones with a heavy, careless rhythm. As soon as their backs turned, we slipped across the open ground, moving fast and low. We disappeared into the long, downhill winding, dirt road leading to the Limani dock in Karlovassi. The dock loomed ahead, old, splintering wood jutting into the dark water. The ferry bobbed at the end, its faded hull groaning with every gentle slap of the waves. Aunt Venetia hissed softly and a figure detached itself from the shadows. It was Uncle Manolis. He didn't say anything. He just waved us forward with a sharp jerk of his chin. A rope ladder dangled over the side of the ferry. Uncle Manolis boosted me up without a word. The ladder swung wildly, the black water yawning below. I climbed, my fingers scraping against the rough rope. At the top, a sailor grabbed my wrist and hauled me aboard, shoving me toward a stack of crates. "Stay there," he muttered. "Don't move."

I crouched behind the crates, my heart pounding so hard I thought it might shake the wooden boxes. From my hiding spot, I saw Mother on the dock, her face pale, but shining in the moonlight. She raised one hand and with a tiny, broken wave, she disappeared into the darkness. I pressed my hand to my lips, sending her a silent kiss. Then, the ferry quivered, groaned, and began to pull away. The gap between us widened. The village shrank into a smudge of shadow and light. The dock fell away into the darkness. The island itself, my whole world, began to disappear into the mist. I buried my face in my knees and cried silently. I did not cry because I was leaving. I cried because I stayed too long. I cried because I was not able to take them all with me. And I cried for not being able to keep my promise, yet.

Chapter 8: Athens

The ferry docked just after dawn. I rose ahead like a monster in the dark into a chaos of broken buildings and shattered dreams. Somewhere in that chaos, I would find a way to grow strong. I would find a way to one day return for all of them. I would go back for them no matter what it cost and no matter how long it took. The gangplank thudded heavily onto the port of Piraeus, the sound of it echoing like a cannon shot in the heavy, salt choked air. I clutched the worn bag that held everything I owned and took my first steps onto the mainland of Greece. It did not look like the Greece I remembered from my schoolbooks or the songs my mother used to sing while weaving in the courtyard. This was a Greece that wore its wounds openly. The city smelled like burnt bread, sewage, and fear. Pale light spread across the crumbling harbor like the fingers of a dying man. Athens, a city bruised and bleeding from war, rose beyond the water in jagged, gray heaps. Bombed out buildings leaned drunkenly against one another. Windows gaped open like broken shells. The marble bones of temples and statues stood shattered among the wreckage. The glories of the ancients were half buried in ash.

I stepped onto the dock, my bundle clutched tight against my chest. My knuckles were white with strain. Around me, the world moved in hungry, desperate tides. Women were wrapped in torn coats, haggling with sharp eyed vendors, selling bruised peaches from splintered crates. Hollow eyed children darted through the crowds like shadows. Men with cigarettes hanging from their lips muttered in tight, secretive knots while their glances were sharp and wary. Soldiers were everywhere. Some soldiers wore the blue and white of the government forces. Others, in ragged, piecemeal uniforms were harder to place. They carried rifles slung across their backs like extra arms while they eyed the crowds like wolves searching for weak prey to tear apart. I kept my head down and moved quickly. No one seemed to notice a thin, dusty girl with old shoes and a patched up dress. I carried only a small bundle in my handkerchief. No one seemed to care.

At a corner where a great building had collapsed into a heap of stone and twisted iron, a man stood on a crate shouting about freedom, about the people's army and about throwing off the chains of tyranny. A soldier cracked him across the face with a rifle butt and dragged him away. The crowd swallowed the scene like it had never happened and I kept walking into the unknown reality of Athens. The coins Mother had given me jingled in my pocket. I needed a way to find my uncle. I needed shelter. I thought of the others, the ones who fought in the mountains, who dreamed of a new Greece, a Greece without kings or tyrants, but I quickly realized that I needed to survive the day.

At the edge of the marketplace I noticed a woman squatted beside a burned out truck, ladling watery stew from a dented pot into chipped cups. I handed her a coin. She eyed me suspiciously but took it, filling a cup with gray broth that smelled faintly of cabbage. I gulped it down so fast it scalded my tongue. Still, my stomach gnawed at itself, unsatisfied. I found a broken bench under a dead tree and sat, wiping my mouth with the back of my hand. The street buzzed full of life and danger around me. Somewhere not far off, a gunshot cracked the air but no one flinched, except me.

I closed my eyes and thought of Lekka. I thought of the hills blooming with wild thyme and of the goats baaing on the rocky slopes. The thought of Mother's warm hands and my brother and sisters sleeping piled together like a litter of puppies made me choke. I would not cry because I had made my choice, a forced choice, but a choice nonetheless. I had left so I could one day return strong enough to lift them all out of the dirt and fear. I was not alone. My uncle was here somewhere, but where? Fighters were everywhere. The ones who had hidden in the mountains during the German occupation, now fought the government itself for a new future. They were here too. Mother had warned me about them in fearful whispers. "They're dreamers, Athena *mou*. (my Athena) Dreamers get shot and get sent to prison camps." Dreams and hope I still had, but now uncertainty weighed heavier than anything else.

I noticed a pair of boys my age loitering near the edge of the port, kicking a dented can between them. Their clothes were rags stitched with rags, but their eyes were sharp and their movements were quick. They glanced at me and then looked away, pretending not to see. I recognized the look, an invitation wrapped in indifference. I stood strong and approached them, every step scraping against my confidence. "Where can I find Petros, the owner of Petros' *Taverna* in the city center of Athens?" I asked.

They both looked at me through flickering emotions, curiosity and calculation. The taller boy had a scar across his eyebrow. His hands were big but his arms were unusually thin. He hesitantly jerked his head toward the ruins of the old church. "It's not far from here. We can show you where it is." I wasn't sure if I trusted them, but I nodded once and followed closely behind them as they started walking off. I had no other option for the moment.

The *taverna* wasn't far from the port, Aunt Venetia had told me, but in the chaos of Athens, nothing felt near. The air smelled of brine and smoke, and a sourness I couldn't place. The streets around the port were choked with people. There were men with sunken cheeks and tattered clothes and women with scarves tightly wound around their hair. Their babies were clutched to their breasts as they walked quickly along the fractured sidewalks. Soldiers leaned against collapsing walls, their eyes scanning the crowd with a cold, glassy indifference that sent a shiver down my spine.

The streets were narrow and unparalleled, like veins in a wounded body. I passed rows of houses, with stone walls broken like brittle bread. They were covered with holes in their sides where mortar shells had landed. Laundry, sometimes nothing more than torn rags, fluttered listlessly in the weak breeze. I tried not to stare at the people huddled in doorways of the broken down shops. Most were wrapped in thin cloth coats. Some of them watched me pass with empty eyes and others didn't even lift their heads. Here and there, children would dart between the rubble. Even their faces were sharp. I saw a little boy who looked like Pavlos crouching next to a ruined fountain, trying to fish something from the stagnant water. My heart warmed when I saw him, but I kept walking.

The sounds of the city were muted somehow. I followed the two boys closely, praying they were guiding me in the right direction. I noticed that there were no songs, no shouting of market vendors and no laughter in these streets heading toward Athens Center. I heard only the occasional crack of a distant gunshot, the mournful clanging of a bell, or the low grumble of army trucks passing on cracked roads. Walls were splashed with graffiti like hurried scrawls. The slogans spoke of freedom, resistance, and vengeance. I could feel the tension crackling in the air, an invisible noose tightening around the city's throat. In the distance, the Acropolis loomed, apathetic and eternal. It felt like a relic from a dead civilization, its grandeur hollow against the backdrop of hunger and fear.

We reached the city center as the sun began to droop low in the sky, shining across the ruined rooftops. My heart skipped a beat when I noticed Uncle Petros' *Taverna* crouched in the shadow of a battered stone building, its sign swinging precariously on a single rusted chain. The smell of boiled beans and roasted chestnuts floated weakly through the door, and my stomach, empty, cramped painfully. I approached the two boys and smiled with sincere gratitude. "Thank you for your help. I don't think I would have been able to find my way here on my own," I said.

"It's our pleasure." the taller boy replied. "You're one of us." I wasn't really sure what he meant or if I would ever see them again, but at this point, I didn't care. I just waved, bowing slightly in gratitude and approached to doorway of Petros' *Taverna*.

Chapter 9: Smoke, Secrets and Loss

Inside, the *taverna* was dim and warm with a single oil lamp throwing long shadows across the cracked floor. Uncle Petros looked older than I remembered, his once black hair was now streaked with gray, and deep lines carved his face. When he saw me, his mouth cracked into a weary smile, and he hurried to pull me into a rough, warm hug. "Welcome, *koritsi mou.*" (my girl) he whispered into my hair, voice thick with emotion. "You made it." I clung to him a moment longer than necessary, breathing in the smell of tobacco, sweat, and wine. For the first time since leaving Samos, I allowed myself to believe that maybe, I would survive this, but even as I stood there, safe for the moment, I felt that this Athens was not a city to be trusted. Every corner and every shadow seemed to hold secrets, alliances, and dangers that I did not yet understand. Here, it seemed, survival meant more than work. It meant watching, listening and keeping your head down. Deep in my soul I felt that survival meant never letting yourself hope too much.

The moon glistened the sky as the evening dragged on. Somewhere, a woman wailed. A dog barked once, sharply, and then fell silent. I pressed my forehead against my knees and whispered the names of my brother and sisters like a prayer, "Aphrodite. Eleni. Christina. Maritza. Pavlos. Katerina. Anna." I would build a world where they never had to sleep in fear again. I nodded off for a minute in the back corner of the *taverna* and for now, I felt safe in the broken city.

I was tired, bone tired, the kind of tired that settles not just in your limbs, but in your soul. My feet ached from the journey, my back was sore, and behind my eyes, throbbed a headache born from too many sleepless nights. More than tired, I was sad. It was a slow, quiet sadness that had been building for months. I missed home, even with all its pain. I missed Mother's voice in the morning, the way the wind sounded over the mountains and through the trees in Lekka. I missed the smell of oregano that clung to the hills at dusk. I missed a version of myself I had left behind, and yet, beneath the exhaustion, beyond the sorrow, I felt something else. I felt a deep, aching kind of gratitude that made my chest feel tight.

I had found Uncle Petros just when I thought the world had forgotten me. I found him when I feared that I might disappear into this cold, unfamiliar place. He didn't ask questions, but he didn't hesitate to open his arms. I had stepped into them like a child coming in from the cold. It wasn't just that he gave me a place to rest, it was that he saw me. That in this foreign land of strange voices and unfamiliar streets, someone remembered who I was and where I came from. That made all the difference. I waited patiently for Uncle Petros to close the *taverna* so that we could go.

We walked through the night to get to Uncle Petros' house. He said that I could work at his *taverna*. His instructions were short, firm and strict. "You will not speak to anyone. The wolves come out at night Athena, and they have an appetite for girls like you. You will withhold your dignity and grace Athena." I quickly nodded. "Yes, Theo Petro."

I lay awake that night, listening to the city breathe. Above me, the cracked ceiling showed signs of wear. In my chest, Mother's voice whispered, *"Athena mou. My brave girl."* I turned onto my side, facing the wall, my eyes burning. I thought of my sisters and brother as a cold tear rolled down my cheek. I thought of Panayiotis and how his hope was beautiful but reckless. I thought of what could have been if I would have escaped to the mountains with him. I then thought of Mother again, and I could not bear the thought of her getting another letter, another knock at the door, another grief that would sink her to her knees. The forced decision to leave the island came not like a thunderclap, but like the slow opening of a door I hadn't known was there. I breathed a slight sigh of relief as I knew that I could not have been the next wound that would have bled my family dry. I was smuggled out of Lekka for my own safety, but I knew that the reason I left was to save them. I refused to be the one to have shattered Mother and my siblings forever. I had decided to take a quiet step into a different future, a future of hope, determination, work and success.

The *taverna* came to life when the sun dipped low and the streets became too dangerous to linger in. At night, the walls breathed with secrets. Uncle Petros' *taverna* was a humble one with its uneven stone floor, a handful of mismatched tables, and oil lamps flickering in dusty corners. A single iron stove warmed the space where the scent of lentil soup, vinegar, and cloves lingered like perfume. There was a yellowed picture of the Virgin Mary above the counter, her face faded, eyes forever tilted toward sorrow. I wiped tables and scrubbed pans, barely speaking unless spoken to. They thought it was shyness, or maybe fear. It made the patrons murmur in hushed tones. I realized that it wasn't just me they whispered about. It was the civil war. It was the war they never spoke of openly, but somehow, always quietly muttered about. Greece was bleeding from the inside.

The Germans had left, but something worse had taken root, a bitter war between the royalist nationalists and the communist resistance fighters. Brother fought brother now. Villages were burned by their own sons. Fathers were arrested by men they once drank with, and no one could be trusted. Athens' center had been a hotbed for the leftists during the Occupation, and everyone knew it. The *taverna* had once fed ELAS fighters, had hidden them in the cellar after they passed notes under plates of stew. Even now, there were looks passed between certain men and heads that dipped lowly together. Hands slid folded pieces of paper across the counter when they thought no one was looking. I saw everything, but I said nothing.

Uncle Petros didn't talk much, but one night, after we had closed and were quietly washing dishes, he looked over and said, "Never look a man too long in the eye, not these days. You never know what side he's on, or what side he thinks you're on." I nodded, the sponge cold in my hand. My fingers were raw from the soap. At night, the *taverna* was lit more by tension than by oil lamps. You could feel it, like a hum in your bones. Men hunched over wine cups with bruised knuckles and dirt under their nails. Women came in wrapped in scarves, eyes darting from one darkened face to the next, hiding children curled beneath their chairs. I saw a young boy no older than Pavlos with a scar down his cheek and a pistol handle jutting from the waistband of his trousers. People came for warmth and sometimes for food, but mostly, they came to listen. They spoke carefully. They gathered names. They came to forget, or to remember, depending on which side they stood on. There were always two or three men who never drank much, were always alone and always listening. The other patrons called them "skies" or "shadows" Their names were never spoken. They were government informants, or so everyone believed. No one dared to ask them directly, but when they entered, conversations shifted like a tide, and silence swallowed the room like fog rolling in off the sea.

Uncle Petros treated everyone the same. He poured the same amount of wine, cut bread in even slices and served lentil soup in the same sized bowl to all that placed their orders. He asked no questions and made no comments. He said it was the only way to survive. "Smile too much, and they think you're hiding something, Frown, and they think you're judging them." he said. "Best to keep your mouth shut and your eyes on the floor." I did as I was told. Still, some patrons began to notice me, "the girl from Samos," they said, "the quiet one who works without complaint and never asks for rest." They called me *"mikri."* (the little one) I heard the whispers. "She's not from around here. She's Petros' niece. She's clean and she doesn't talk. Maybe she can carry a note…" But Uncle Petros always stood nearby, and no one dared ask directly. One night, a group of young partisans came in. They were muddy from the mountains. They had the look of ghosts, with tired eyes, dirty coats and faces too old for their years. Among them was a girl, no older than me, her hair hacked short like a boy's with a rifle slung over her back. They sat in the corner, their shoulders brushing, sharing cigarettes and quiet laughter. I brought them their food and tried not to stare, but something about them gripped me. They looked like freedom, wild, broken, dangerous freedom. It was a reminder of what I had nearly become, of Panyiotis and of the road not taken. That road was no longer mine. I had made my choice, and every day I worked in the *taverna*. With every plate I washed and every floor I swept, I felt the ache of that choice like a slow aching pain spreading through my ribs. Sometimes, I wondered what Panayiotis was doing and whether he still walked the hills of Samos with his rifle in hand and the red star stitched to his sleeve. I wondered whether he still thought of me, or whether he had already forgotten the girl who couldn't choose him over her family.

The midday sun beat down on the narrow streets of Athens, warming the marble step outside Uncle Petro's home. The city bustled with the noise of street vendors and the endless shouts of children playing in alleyways. Inside my cool, shaded room everything felt eerily still. I sat on the edge of my cot, smoothing the hem of my skirt with absent fingers. I had just come back from the farmer's market and my woven bag, still half full with tomatoes and onions, lay on the floor beside me. I was reaching to unlace my shoes when the landlady appeared in the doorway. "There's a letter for you," she said, holding out an envelope with careful reverence. I took it, hopeful it would bring good news. I knew it was from Pavlos. I recognized the slope of his letters and the way he looped the capital A in my name as if protecting it. I opened it immediately. Slowly and carefully, my fingers fumbled with the edge of the paper, unfolding the letter with a weight in my chest that threatened to crush me before the words ever reached my eyes.

Athena mou,

Yiayia Athena passed yesterday. She waited until they placed your photograph in her hands. Her breathing was shallow for days, and her body was so thin she seemed barely there. She held on as if she was waiting for something, waiting for someone. When Mother slid your photograph into her palms, she let go. Her last breath was deep, like a sigh after a long journey. Her eyes, which had been dull and distant for weeks, lit up for a moment. Then she closed her eyes for the last time, let out a slight sigh and a half smile on her face. I know how much you loved her. She loved you more.

The letter dropped to my lap. The rest of the letter was blurred. It held details of the burial, who attended, how Lekka square had quieted when the bells tolled, but none of it mattered to me in that moment. My shoulders hunched forward as if I'd been struck. The room spun slightly, and the world outside, the market, the sun, and the sound of children fell away. My breath came in sharp, uneven bursts. I pressed the letter to my chest and doubled over, my forehead touching my knees. I tried to hold in the sound of my grief, but I could not. *"NO!"* I hollered, a whale so profound that it resonated into the streets of Athens.

Yiayia Athena had been my constant confident. She was my whisper of hope. She was a silent warrior in a village that worshiped silence for women. She had seen me, not just as a child, but as a future, a future better than hers. I could see *Yiayia* in her illness now. Pavlos had described it well. Unbidden tears came to my eyes. I pictured *Yiayia*'s deep, sunken eyes rimmed with the gray of suffering and her fingers curling in on themselves, blue at the tips from poor circulation. I could hear my *Yiayia*'s breath, shallow and rattling, while her chest rose and fell like an exhausted tide. I saw *Yiayia*'s jaw clenched with pain, and her expression softening only when my photograph was placed in her hand. *Yiayia* had waited for me. She needed me near, even in just my photo, to die in peace.

I pressed my lips to the letter and let the tears fall freely onto the ink. My cries were muffled, but my heart screamed. I wasn't there to comfort her, to brush the damp hair from her wrinkled brow or kiss her goodbye. I wasn't there to say thank you, to whisper all the things I'd learned from her. I tried to take solace in the fact that she knew how much she meant to me. I know that *Yiayia* had understood because she sent me a message from her death bed. *Yiayia*'s death, with my face in her hand, was her final message, *I believe in you, my favorite Athena. Now go.* The letter, now slightly crumpled in my fist, was damp with tears. The paper trembled as if it too, could feel my sorrow. I leaned my head back against the wall and shut my eyes.

Yiayia's face came to me then, not in death, not pale and gaunt in the bed Pavlos had described, but full of life, bathed in the light of a Samos afternoon. I was back in Lekka, about ten years old. The dust had kicked up after Father slammed the front door behind himself, and we had scattered like frightened cats. I had run down the stone path behind the trees, wiping tears from my cheeks with the back of my hand. My feet were cracked and dry. I had no shoes on, only calluses and stubbornness carried me forward. I ran until she reached *Yiayia* Athena's doorstep. My grandmother had been sitting in her usual spot on the worn wooden stool, peeling apples into a wide enamel basin. She said nothing when she saw me approach, she just opened her arms. I fell into her lap. *Yiayia* smelled of cinnamon and her hands felt like silk against my tangled hair. She didn't ask questions. She didn't need to. Instead, *Yiayia* hummed that low, ancient melody, the one passed down from mothers to daughters. It had no words, just notes that sounded like the ocean. Then she moved her lips close to my ear to say, "You are not small *koukla mou* (my doll). You are the wild fig tree that grows even in stone."

I looked up. "But I'm not strong like Pavlos. I am not a boy."

"You are stronger," *Yiayia* Athena had looked at me with her sharp, yet soft eyes and said, "He protects, but you… you will change everything."

Now, in my tiny room in Athens, I clutched that memory like the last thread in a tapestry. The ache of loss spread wide in my chest, but beneath it was something else, something sturdy. I may have not been there to hold *Yiayia*'s hand as she slipped away, but *Yiayia* had held mine even as she passed. She had held me for a lifetime.

I stood up slowly, folded the letter and placed it under my pillow. I lit the oil lamp by the window in *Yiayia*'s memory, then bowed my head in prayer and in promise. "I will change everything, *Yiayia*, just like you said I could." I whispered. "Even if the whole world says I can't. I will." Outside, the bells of a nearby chapel began to chime. The sound rose into the twilight air, as if calling the soul of a wise old woman up into the stars.

Chapter 10: The Mountains Took Them

In Lekka tradition clung tightly to the bones of the land. Samos' customs were like vines around old stone walls that refused to loosen their grip. For generations, marriages had been arranged with care, negotiated with pride and approved only with a father's solemn nod. But Eleni and Aphrodite were not girls who fit easily into molds carved by other hands.

Eloping was not uncommon in the hills and forests of Samos, especially in the years after the war. Girls feared being married off by force. It was a custom as old as the soil itself. If a young man wanted a girl, and the girl returned his interest, but the family did not approve, they found a secret way to consummate their love. They ran into the olive groves, into the mountains and into whatever darkness offered. The mountains were the shelter of love. Once they escaped into the mountains, and a girl had lain with a boy, even just once, there was no going home. She was, by village standards, *damaged*. She belonged to him now.

It began with Eleni. with her fiery eyes that always looked past the horizon. She had always been wild hearted. Her laughter rang through the groves like wind chimes stirred by a summer breeze. She had long been in love with Christos, a tough, sharp eyed boy from the village. Christos too, had fallen in love with Eleni when they were children. They chased goats up the mountain paths, daring each other to leap from rocks. By the time they were old enough to speak of marriage, their bond had grown too deep to untangle. Christos was the young mason with hands rough from stone and a heart as tender as the bread his mother baked every Sunday. Everyone in Lekka knew of their secret love. Neighbors whispered it behind trees and stalls, but for Father, love was not enough. Christos was poor. He was honest and hardworking, but he had no land, and no dowry to speak of.

When Eleni gathered the courage to speak to Father, he dismissed her with a thunderous glare and a slammed door. Unyielding and proud, Father refused. Christos' family had few prospects and a history stained by political whispers. "A marriage must bring strength," Father declared. "Not more mouths to feed." Eleni didn't argue. "You will not waste yourself on a stone cutter," he said. "You will marry where I say, and no one else." But Eleni, for all her gentle demeanor, carried something unbreakable in her spirit. She simply disappeared one evening, under a silver moon, with Christos, the love of her life.

The air was thick with pine the night Eleni left. She moved like a shadow through the yard, her boots tied around her neck to soften her steps. She wore only a simple dress and a woolen shawl over her shoulders. Her dark braid was tucked into a scarf. She paused under the fig tree where she and Christos had kissed for the first time. Her heart was pounding, but she didn't look back. Christos was waiting at the edge of the path. His face lit up when he saw her, but he said nothing. He took her hand, and they ran. They darted up the hill, past the church and into the shadows of the mountains. The moon spilled silver on the rocks and nothing could follow them but fate. They walked for hours in silence, their breath clouding in the cold. Near the shepherd's cave, an old priest, once a partisan himself, waited with a rusted cross and trembling hands. He had known Christos since he was a boy. He said the prayers with reverence, and when the ceremony was done, he placed a single olive branch at their feet. "You've made your choice," the priest said. "Now, carry it like a banner."

Mother didn't cry. She simply stopped talking for days. Her heart was torn between relief that Eleni had escaped Father's hand and grief that she might never see her again. Three days later, the couple returned to Lekka as husband and wife. They were sun burnt, dusty, ragged and proud. Eleni's braid was wind blown and her cheeks ruddy from the climb, but her eyes glowed with the steel of a woman who had chosen her path. She stood beside Christos. Their hands were tightly entwined, and she wore a plain gold band on her finger. They walked into the yard without fear. Father stood still in the doorway, his jaw clenched, but he said nothing. He only turned his back. They got no blessing that day, no feast, and father didn't speak to them for months. Several months later, Christos built a modest whitewashed home on the hill above the terraces, and Eleni filled it with laughter. They had one child, whose gaze sparkled with something unspoken, like she was born with the memory of the night her mother had defied everything for love.

A few weeks later, Aphrodite followed. Her elopement was bolder and more defiant. Aphrodite would rather sleep on stones than bow to a man like Father. Dionisios was known for his politics, a rebel sympathizer who refused to attend church. When Eleni disappeared, the village gossiped for weeks, their tongues sharp as blades. This didn't stop Aphrodite. If Eleni's rebellion was a spark, Aphrodite's was a flame. Aphrodite had watched it all, quietly absorbing the scandal, the defiance, and the bittersweet freedom that came after Eleni eloped. She had fallen in love too, though Aphrodite's story was more dangerous. Although she was the eldest, she was not as brave as Eleni. Aphrodite too was in love with someone she knew Father would never accept.

Aphrodite had closely watched her sister's defiance. Her love, Dionisios, was much more dangerous than Christos. He was not just poor. Dionisios was a rebel, marked by the war. A boy turned man too quickly, he had taken to the hills with the partisans, fighting first against the fascists, then the royalists, and finally perhaps, against fate itself. Dionisios had come to Lekka only to see Aphrodite slipping through shadows like a ghost. He brought stories of comrades fallen, of betrayal, survival, and of hope, however fragile it was. He was marked from the civil war, had fled conscription, and bore scars that never healed. But Aphrodite saw in Dionisios something no one else did. Even when Father insisted, "He's a communist. Over my dead body!" Aphrodite saw a gentleness beneath the armor, a hunger for peace that only love could feed. "He's a criminal, a hunted man. He'll bring death to our doorstep. I'd sooner see you dead in the ground," Father growled.

Where Eleni had run away in the night, Aphrodite stood her ground in daylight. Her eyes blazed with determination. Her heart belonged to Dionisios, the brooding boy who had talked of freedom, of justice and of a Greece that could breathe again. Dionisios didn't ask for permission. He fought for what he believed in and Aphrodite loved him for it. One morning, just before the first frost, Aphrodite left before the roosters crowed.

She took nothing but a handkerchief and a loaf of bread. Aphrodite climbed through the foothills to a rebel hideout where Dionisios waited, his eyes scanning the horizon for both danger and her face. She didn't speak. She simply placed her hand in his and nodded. That was all it took. They were married before sunrise. Rumors spread by noon. By dusk, the whole of Lekka knew. Aphrodite had eloped.

Aphrodite and Dionisios returned to Lekka without apology and without shame. There was no fanfare, only silence and the disapproving stares of villagers who feared the world beyond the hills. Aphrodite's face was calm and her spine was straight with pride. Dionisios, though tired from a life of fighting, stood taller with her beside him. But their return was brief. Dionisios had joined the *andartes*, (the Greek freedom fighters) battling in the rugged hills for their ideals. With civil war swelling around them, Aphrodite loved and followed him wherever he went. Their lives were built in the shadows of struggle, in cold camps and whispered prayers. Somehow, they still built a family. Dionisios and Aphrodite had four children, strong, wild, and full of questions. Dionisios never left the struggle completely. He worked the land by day, but at night, his stories were of comrades and freedom, of betrayals and victories, half won. He became known throughout the region as a freedom fighter. Some said he was dangerous. Others said he was necessary, and through it all, the two sisters, Eleni and Aphrodite, remained unshakable. Married not by Father's standards, but by passion, bound not by duty, but by courage.

Eleni, more rooted, stayed in Lekka. She and Christos carved a life from the soil, their home filled with laughter and their courtyard with lemon trees. They had one daughter, a radiant girl with jet black hair that fell like silk down her back. Her eyes were the color of a winter sky, baby blue and impossibly bright. They sparked and shone with mischief, joy and a light, so pure, even Father could not ignore when she toddled through his yard. Father never spoke of the weddings that didn't happen in his house, but sometimes, when he thought no one was looking, he smiled at the child with the starlight eyes.

The mountains had taken Eleni and Aphrodite, but both had eventually returned, women forged by love and defiance, and not even Father could undo what had been done. The sisters who defied their father became women of their own making. They were not married by permission, but by choice. In the village square, the old women still shook their heads sometimes, but time dulled the edges of scandal.

Chapter 11: Silence and Whispers

The letter came on a Tuesday, thin and smudged, with the familiar script that made Athena cringe. She turned it over in her hands before opening it, as if she could sense the weight of what it carried before she even read a word. It was from Christina.

Athena mou,

I write with shaky hands. The village is quieter now, but not in peace. It is the quiet of those who are too afraid to speak. Too many things are happening behind closed doors.

Athena's eyes moved quickly, searching for the part she already feared was coming.

There is still no word of Panayiotis. Some say he was captured outside of Patras. Others whisper he was taken to the prison on Makronisos. But I heard from Stelios, the butcher's son, that he swears he saw Panayioti on a ship in Thessaloniki. He says he wore a French soldier's coat, boarded with a false name. Athena, could it be? Could he be alive?

Athena's hands shook. She had imagined Panayiotis in so many forms, bloodied, lost, wandering, but still alive and starting over? That hope was more dangerous than grief.

And Athena, there is something else.

She paused.

You may already know, but I must tell you plainly. Persefoni has also disappeared. She just vanished. One morning she was gone, and no one saw her leave. Some say she went mad after the second child. Others claim Father sent her away to keep the rumors from spreading further. But the talk has only grown worse. I don't know what is true, but Eleni said something that chilled me. She said she once saw Father slip a small bag into a stranger's hand beneath the old fig tree. That same week, the baker was gone too. Some think he and Persefoni ran off together. Others believe something darker happened. Something no one dares say aloud.

Athena pressed the letter to her chest, the paper damp against her skin. Her heart beat fast, part fury, part fear.

Mother does not speak of any of this, though I know she knows. She has taken to praying loudly in the mornings, as if louder prayers might silence the village.

We miss you. The children ask about Athens and if it's true that your rain shines like salt. Write soon. Tell us you are well.

With love, always,

Christina

Athena folded the letter slowly, then sat in silence. A thin coil of smoke curled toward the ceiling as the candle beside her bed burned low. Outside, the Athens streets lay blanketed in moonlight, but in her mind, she saw only Lekka and the trees swaying under the weight of secrets. She imagined the cold silence of Mother and the empty space where Panayiotis once stood. Athena sat on the edge of her narrow bed, the letter clenched in her hand. Her room was almost dark as the shutters closed against the evening chill. The stove hadn't been lit that night. She didn't move. She just sat there, staring at the words until they blurred into a kaleidoscope of shapes. She remembered Panayiotis not as a ghost or a rumor, but as he had been the last time she saw him, laughing, arms flung wide in the village square, dust on his boots and a burning fire in his eyes. He had argued with Father, with the mayor and with the priest. "If we don't fight now," he had said, "we'll be crawling the ground forever." He never bent, not for anyone. For that, Athena had loved him in the quiet way one loves someone they know will never belong to them. Now he was gone, and she was in Athens, quietly washing dishes and scrubbing floors in Uncle Petros' *taverna*.

She rose slowly and opened the shutters. Outside, rain had begun to fall, soft and aimless. The street below was empty. The wind carried a smell of burning coal and gun smoke.

I didn't go, Athena thought. *I didn't fight.* It wasn't shame she felt. She had made her choice. While Panayiotis took to the mountains, she took to Athens, to the unmarked hours of work and duty and to the silence of sacrifice. She had chosen survival, hers and her family's. She had chosen to live, to endure, to send money back across the sea to keep the children in shoes and the cupboards from going bare. Sometimes, when she read the names of the dead and missing, she wondered what it would have felt like to carry a rifle through the ravines of Samos, to sleep beside Panayiotis under pine boughs and stars and to stand for something more than survival. The world she had chosen was quieter, less heroic, but no less hard.

Perhaps he was dead. Perhaps he was in some prison in Athens, nameless and forgotten. Or perhaps he sat in a cafe in Marseilles now, speaking broken French and watching ships in the harbor, waiting for someone from home to find him. Athena pressed her forehead to the glass. She whispered his name once, softly, as if it might carry across the ocean. "Panayiotis." She hoped he knew that whatever had happened to him, someone still remembered him and that someone, somewhere, still waited for his story to return. Was he truly alive? Had he escaped like she never dared to try? And Persefoni, where had she gone? Who had taken her? Athena moved to the wall and leaned her head against it. Her eyes were burning with the vision of her village. The distance had not severed her from its grief. If anything, it had only deepened the ache. She whispered once more into the air, "Panayioti, if you're out there, come back. Or let me know you're free." But the silence that answered held no promises. She sat there, quietly, wrapped in an old woolen blanket, her hands still tired from the day's work. The single candle beside her flickered for a few more minutes. It cast shadows that seemed to dance with her memories of Panayiotis before its light went out, leaving Athena in complete darkness.

Panayiotis' name sat heavily in her chest. Her mind had refused to let him go. The boy who had once run barefoot through Lekka's groves daring the world to stop him, was now reduced to rumor and whispers. Was he missing, imprisoned, dead, or had he vanished into the gray anonymity of exile? The village of Lekka had always been filled with stories, but not many stung Athena like this one.

And with his name came another, Persefoni, his sister, with her dark curls and sly smile, who once sang at the village festivals. She was the one who always knew where to find the first ripe figs. Persefoni's shadow now loomed over every whispered conversation that drifted through Lekka. Athena could still see her, strutting in the spring sun, walking past the well with a basket slung over one hip and an apron tied tight across her belly. She had always worn her apron, even on the hottest days. It was always full of fruit or herbs, as if hiding something behind the weight of the harvest. Everyone had noticed how she began to move differently. She walked slower, as though balancing something more delicate than oranges. Two pregnancies, they said. Two children born in secret, far from the eyes of the church and the scorn of the old women who watched from behind lace curtains. A girl first, then a boy, both whisked away to distant villages. No names. No baptisms. Just rumors of a boy with Pavlos' chin and the same hazel eyes. They spoke of a girl with the same crooked smile as little Anna, whose cry had echoed through the hills for just one night before she was gone.

The stories twisted like vines. Some said Father had been seen slipping into Persefoni's garden at dusk to send her away. Others claimed he lingered too long outside her window during mass, waiting to help her leave. And still, others swore it was the baker, the stout, flour dusted man with arms like hams who had also been visiting her late at night with baskets of warm bread and things far more intentional than kindness. Athena didn't know what to believe. But she knew how the village worked. Truth, lies and rumors danced too closely to separate, and the truth was often bent under the weight of the speaker's own perception.

Athena's thoughts drifted to her mother. Poor Mother, walking through the village with her head held high, skirts freshly ironed and a smile carefully stitched into place. She pretended she didn't hear the laughter behind her and made it look like she hadn't noticed the silence that fell whenever she entered a room. She was the wife of Father and the mother of eight. She was the one everyone mocked, and pitied even more.

Athena's hands curled into fists while she remembered Panayiotis. She had chosen a different kind of battle, a quiet one, waged with sacrifice, silence and rags. Now, she wondered which war had left the deeper wounds. Lekka had its ghosts, and Persefoni's were still alive, roaming the hills, crying out in the wind that blew through the branches. Two children born of shame and silence, a possible brother and sister, now gone without a trace. Athena closed her eyes and prayed, not to the God Father served, but to something older and gentler. She prayed to the God *Yiayia* Athena whispered to in the fields. She prayed for her sisters, her brother, for Panayiotis, and for Mother, who tried to walk tall through a world of whispers. And she prayed for herself too, because the burden of knowing was heavy, and there was no apron big enough to hide this knowledge.

Chapter 12: Unwelcome Hands, Unforgiving Eyes

It was late, the kind of late where the oil lamps hung low with smoke and wine fueled untold stories. The *taverna* was full that night. A storm had rolled in over the Piraeus Port driving sailors, workers, and partisans indoors. Thunder grumbled somewhere above the hills of Athens, and the rain slapped the windows like a warning. I kept to my work, collecting empty cups, wiping down tables, avoiding eyes like I always did. I was swift, polite, and as always, invisible. That was the way you stayed safe as a young woman in a place like this. "Like smoke," Uncle Petros had said, "maybe seen, but never touched." That night, someone tried. He was a tall man, almost too tall for his chair. His hair was slicked back, his cheeks sunken and his eyes glassy with drink. He had been laughing loudly all night, slapping the backs of comrades, telling stories about the mountains and the "glorious hunt for traitors." The others didn't laugh with him. They drank and kept their mouths shut.

When I bent to gather his empty plate, I felt it, a rough and sudden hand on the back of my thigh. I froze. My breath caught like a needle dragging across vinyl. He grinned up at me with yellowed teeth. "What's a girl like you doing here, eh? Pretty face like yours, you could feed soldiers something sweeter than soup." His breath stank of retsina. "Sit with me. Come. You look lonely."

I stepped back quickly my heart hammering. "I have work to do," I said flatly, keeping my voice calm and controlled. He reached again, bolder this time, grabbing my wrist with determination and force. "Uncle Petros!" I cried, louder than I intended.

Before the man could say another word, Uncle Petros was there, a flash of fury in his normally impassive face. His hands came down hard on the man's shoulder. "Get your hands off her."

The man sneered. "Easy old man. She's working in a *taverna*, not a monastery."

Uncle Petros didn't flinch. "She's my niece and this isn't that kind of place." The tension in the room thickened. Chairs scraped the floor. Conversations stopped. Curious and wary eyes turned towards us. The skies, the secret informants who always lingered in the corners glanced over, noting everything. "Out," Uncle Petros growled. "Now."

The man stood up, his eyes unsteady and narrowing. "You think she'll last long out here with that face? You're naive old man. The wolves are hungry."

Uncle Petros didn't reply. He just stood there, frozen strong, until the man finally stumbled out into the storm. Later that night, after the lamps were doused and the doors bolted, we sat alone in the kitchen. The silence between us was thick. Uncle Petros poured coffee, but neither of us drank it. "He touched you," he finally said. I nodded. "It's over." He looked at me with sorrow in his eyes, but also a strange kind of relief like he had finally made a decision he had been dreading. "You can't stay here, *kopela mou.* (my girl) It's no place for you. You're not just any girl from Athens. You're an island girl from a good family, your mother's daughter."

"I can handle myself," I said eagerly hoping I could somehow change Uncle Petro's mind.

"I know you can, but your father..." He sighed. "If he finds out, he'll blame your mother and they will all pay. He'll say I let wolves near you. He'll never forgive that."

I clenched my fists under the table. A thousand protests flooded my chest. I was careful. I worked hard. I kept my head down but none of that mattered now. One man and his hand had erased it all.

He continued gently, "You've done more than enough. It's time to think bigger than this *taverna*. You were meant for more than scrubbing wine from stone floors. You're not like them." His voice cracked, barely audible. "And I won't have you ruined."

My throat was tight, but I managed to swallow before speaking. "I didn't come to Athens to hide." I whispered.

"No," he said, "You came to save yourself and your family." He was right, but still, my heart ached, not just from the man's hand, or the fear, but from the bitter truth. I didn't belong anywhere, not here, not in the mountains, not even in the warmth of Uncle Petros' quiet kitchen. I was a girl stitched together, surrounded by the twirls of life and Father's curse. I had no choice but to keep going.

In the gray light of early morning, I gathered my few things and decided to explore the city in hopes of finding work. I stood up, brushed the dust from my shoes, and walked toward the old church. The city was waking up as I wandered the broken streets. Vendors set up battered stalls, laying out wilted vegetables and scraps of cloth. Soldiers leaned against walls, rifles slung lazily over their shoulders. The ruins wore their wounds in the morning sun, like old scars. At a bakery near the market square, I saw a sign nailed neatly on the door, *Live-in maid wanted. Room and board included.* I stared at it for a long moment. My heart skipped a couple of beats. I desperately needed this job. I clenched my fists with determination. Then, I slowly knocked on the door.

The house was old but proud, tucked between two broken apartment buildings on a narrow street. The woman who opened the door had tired eyes. She smiled kindly, studied me for a moment, then ushered me inside. I kept my head bowed as she asked questions, my name, my island and my age. When she asked if I could cook and clean, I quickly nodded. "Anything. I will do anything!" She instantly pressed a rough cloth apron into my hands and led me to a tiny room under the stairs.

The bed was no more than a cot. The walls were grayish stone, but to me it looked like a kingdom. I sank onto the cot, the weight of my luck settling over me like a blanket. I did not feel like a fighter. I was no goddess of war at that moment. I was just a girl who was determined to make a better life for herself, and for her family. I wanted to live, to work, and to make something of the pieces I had been given. For now, I was lucky to have found this woman and was determined to serve her well.

It was a few weeks later that I met him. Dimitri came to the house to tutor the family's youngest son, a boy too frail to go out into the dangerous city streets. I saw him first through the kitchen window, his worn bag slung over one shoulder, a book tucked under his arm. He walked like a man used to dodging rubble, his head bowed slightly as if carrying invisible weight. When he smiled at the boy, it was like the sun breaking through a storm. He seemed gentle, steady, safe and true. He was nothing like Panayiotis, no reckless wildness, no burning anger. He displayed a quiet, stubborn belief that knowledge could rebuild what war had broken.

Over time, Dimitri started to notice me. At first, he gestured a polite nod, and murmured *"Kalimera"* (Good morning) in passing as I scrubbed the floor or carried laundry. Then, his glances became longer and more concentrated. We started sharing small conversations that were never improper or dangerous. We shared respectful words, carefully placed like stones across a river. He asked about my island. I told him about Lekka's thyme scented hills, the sunsets, the goats and the sea. For once in my life, the heaviness of my heart felt lifted and free. I finally felt safe.

Dimitri asked about my family, and I spoke of my brother and sisters with pride. He never asked about the scars and I didn't speak of them. He never pried into the silences I couldn't yet fill. Instead, he told me about poetry, about Sappho, Seferis and Elytis. He entertained me with words stitched with light, sorrow, life and hope. He read to me in the afternoons, his voice low and even, and for the first time in my life, I believed that the world could be built not just with guns and fists, but with the beauty of words. I understood that knowledge could be a kind of armor, that love could be kind and revolution may not be welcomed.

I missed Panayiotis sometimes. I missed the flame that once kept me warm even as it scorched me. I missed the way he made me feel, alive and reckless, but I did not miss the fear. I did not miss the constant edge of death. Mother's voice was right. Dreams could be beautiful, but some dreams needed to be burned not tended to.

Dimitri never made my heart race in terror. He made it steady, like a hand pressed against your back, holding you upright when the world tried to push you down. I barely noticed it happening, but I slowly began to fall in love. Not the wild, desperate love of a girl clinging to escape and survival, but the patient, rooted love of a girl choosing a future, choosing hope and choosing life. I admired Dimitri's knowledge and listened carefully to his words. I loved that he was smart. He read words of beauty, hope and praise. He was everything I could never have been because I was never given the chance to.

I only made it as far as second grade. I remember the classroom in Lekka, small, drafty, with cracked plaster walls and wooden benches that creaked every time someone shifted their weight. I loved it there. I loved the smell of chalk and ink and the rhythm of learning. I truly enjoyed the way my teacher would smile when I read aloud without stumbling. Letters felt like magic to me, like little doors to places I hadn't seen yet. But just as I was starting to read with confidence, just as numbers began to make sense, Father said I was done. "You've learned enough," he told me, without even looking me in the eye. "You can read, you can write. That's all a girl like you needs. The fields are calling." And that was that. There was no argument to be had. No one asked what I wanted, not even Mother. She wouldn't dare to.

Father had decided that only Katerina and Pavlos would keep going to school. Pavlos of course, because he was a boy and a man in the making. He needed an education, Father said, "so he could make something of himself." And Katerina because she was the clever one, always better in school than the rest of us. Even Father could see that. He said it would be a waste not to let her continue. But me? I was strong. I was good with a spade and I knew how to coax a sprout from hard earth. So I was the one who stayed behind. The one who tilled and turned soil while Katerina and Pavlos carried books. I dug the trenches for potatoes, planted rows of onions and beans, hauled buckets of water from the well until my arms went numb. Father said I was made for it, 'like an ox or a mule." He often used those words.

While I broke my back under the sun, Father roamed the hills. Sometimes he'd disappear for whole afternoons, drinking or chasing after Persefoni, the widow who always wore too much perfume. We all knew where he went. We just never dared say it aloud. It hurt to be left behind, not just from school, but from the possibility of something more. I remember watching Katerina walk to class in her clean dress, books tied with a bit of twine. I remember feeling a sour twist in my belly. It was not envy, just a dull ache, like I'd been forgotten and like I didn't matter as much. But I never cried, not once. Instead, I buried the ache, the longing, and I learned to keep my head down. I learned to work harder than anyone and to be useful, because in our house, that was the only way to be seen.

Chapter 13: A Letter for a Blessing

Life settled into a hard, steady and familiar rhythm. I woke before the sun, scrubbed floors until my knees ached, washed linens until my fingers cracked from the lye soap. I learned to sew, to mend, to bake the bread that kept their household running. Every coin I earned, every half drachma, every worn bill, I tucked carefully into a tin under my cot. Once a month, when the ferries made their way back to Samos, I sent almost all of it home. I sent almost everything I earned to Mother, to Pavlos and to my sisters who were still sleeping on those same sagging mattresses and still swallowing their cries in the dark. A few crumpled notes tucked into the folds of a letter read, *"Buy flour. Buy shoes for the little ones. Take Mother to the doctor if you can."* I sent hope folded into envelopes. For me, it was love sent across the sea. I kept almost nothing for myself. I spent only what was needed to buy a secondhand dress when my apron fell to rags, or a worn book to teach myself the proper Greek letters Dimitri used. It was not much, but it was my dignity.

Dimitri noticed. He noticed the way my hands stayed busy even in the quiet moments and the way my eyes always watched the horizon, as if measuring the distance back to Lekka. He began to leave little gifts where he knew I would find them. He never left anything that would shame me. His presents were like careful and reverent prayers that made me smile. His gifts were small, full of thought and preparation. I found things like a paper flower folded from a discarded book page, a ribbon the color of the sea, a pencil and sometimes, a scrap piece of paper with a heart drawn on it. He never left anything grand but I treasured each and every gift. We spoke often, now. We whispered by the kitchen door, in the gardens and once, even beneath the gnarled arms of an ancient tree where the air smelled of sun and earth. He read me real poems about longing, exile and about patient love that did not demand, it waited. Sometimes, even just a whisper of contact, just the barest of grazes like when his hand brushed mine, my heart would stutter.

In my world, a woman's name was stitched to her honor like embroidery to cloth. You could not tear one without ruining the other. And so we remained, two souls circling, aching, yearning, but never crossing the sacred line, and somehow, that made it all the more precious and bearable. I was Athena of Lekka, daughter of the island, daughter of suffering and pride and I could not, nor would I, offer myself, not even to a man as good and kind as Dimitri.

One evening, as the sun burned itself out against the hills, Dimitri caught my hand fully and boldly. I gasped, not from fear, but from the shock of it. He knelt in the dusty path before me, his voice shaking with something too big for him to hold in. "Athena *mou*," (my Athena) he said, his voice raw. "You are stronger than stone. You are more faithful than the saints. Be my wife. Let me build a life with you, piece by piece."

Tears stung my eyes. I wanted nothing more in that moment than to say yes, to fold myself into the life he offered like a bird finding a home after too many winters. But even then, even in that moment of ultimate sweetness, I knew the road was not yet mine to choose, because life, as it often did, had other plans. The swirls of unsettled dust, the ones that followed me from the island, made me squint in pain. I did not answer Dimirti that night.

The letter came a week later, a thick envelope, the ink smudged from its journey. Father Marcus, the priest from our village, had written it himself.

"Dearest Athena,"

"There is an opportunity for a good and honest girl like you. Canada is taking in girls of good standing to work and build a life

here. I will sponsor you. You will have a place at my parish in Montreal. A chance at a future, better than what the war has left behind. Speak to your family. Pray on it. Decide with care."

I sat at the tiny kitchen table, the letter in my hands. A future across the oceans. A new life in a land of snow and strangers, and a chance not just to survive, but to thrive. I thought of Mother's tired face, the new lines etched by worry. I thought of Pavlos who was almost a man now, his shoulders broadening under burdens no boy should bear. I thought of my sisters, still girls and still dreaming. I thought of Dimitri, his hands, his heart, his hope, and the life I could have with him here in Athens. My chest ached with the weight of this letter. I was torn between the love I had found and the duty that still bound me. Was this letter and the sponsorship from Father Marcus a sign? Was it the push I didn't want right now, but needed? I did the only thing I could. I sat down at the rickety table, pulled a piece of the good paper Dimitri had given me, and began to write.

"Dearest Father,"

"I seek your blessing."

"I feel that I have found love, a wonderful, educated man here in Athens who has proposed marriage. However, there is a chance for me to go to Canada. Father Marcus wrote that he can sponsor

me, and help me find work and a life there. I will not go if it is against your will. My heart tells me to marry Dimitri, but I am a daughter and a sister first. I set out with the wish to help my family and to make sure my sisters and brother never go to sleep with howling stomachs. I want to help my family escape the war, the danger and finally prosper, but my heart has found someone worthy of my love, faith and trust. Perhaps this is God's wish for me to have a better future?"

"Please tell me what you wish of me."

My hand shook as I folded the letter, not from fear, but from the knowledge that no matter what answer came, yes or no, I would need to obey, because that was who I was. I was the daughter that Mother had raised me to be, not wild, not reckless, but faithful and honorable. I knew that I was Athena of Lekka. I was the daughter of stone, salt and sea, but somewhere, deep inside me, I secretly prayed for myself. I needed his blessing, and I also needed to feel loved. Dimitri showed me a gentle love, a kind side of life, like the one that Mother always spoke about, but never could have with Father.

"Let him free me. Let him give me his blessing, and let me go. Either way, any way, let him finally give me the blessing I so desperately need."

I knew what my heart wished for and what I prayed for. I needed an answer that would soothe my heart and my soul. I prayed to do away with the pain of that curse, the curse of swirling dust beneath my feet set upon me by Father himself. I sealed the envelope and whispered a prayer over it before sending it on its way. Then, I waited for the answer that would shape the rest of my life. Would Father encourage me to follow my heart, or enforce my unshakable duty to my family? Would he provide me with the blessing I so desperately needed? I waited patiently for Father's letter because that's all I could do.

Chapter 14: The Letters, The Queen

A letter arrived one dusky morning. The paper was thin and folded into quarters. Its edges were worn and creased. The handwriting was Aphrodite's, elegant, slanted, but more shivering than Athena remembered. She tore it open with shaky fingers.

My beloved sister,

Dionisios has been taken. They came at night, men in khaki uniforms armed with rifles and the stench of fear. The children were screaming. I begged them Athena. I fell to my knees and clutched their boots. But they would not listen. They said he was a communist. A danger. A traitor to the Crown. I do not know where they've taken him. Some say to the island prisons, others to Makronisos. I don't know what to tell my children. I turn to you as I know that you are in Athens.

I beg you, do something. Help us.

With all my heart,

Aphrodite

Athena dropped the letter. Her vision swam. She grabbed the edge of the folding table to steady herself. The room spun with dread, fury and helplessness. Dionisios was taken, kind, loving Dionisios, who loved poetry and carved wooden toys for his children. A man who had fought against the Nazis, who had joined the resistance in the mountains not for ideology, but for freedom. He had been removed from his family and his life, and now, like thousands of others, he had been labeled an enemy. The civil war had fractured the soul of the country. The British backed royalists, desperate to maintain control, had begun purging anyone even suspected of leftist sympathies. Veterans of the EAM-ELAS, the very resistance that had fought against fascism, were now hunted. Accusations flew like bullets. Neighbors turned on neighbors. The prisons overflowed. To be called a communist, true or not, was to be condemned. The names Makronisos. Ai Stratis. Gyaros, places of exile in Greece, sent shivers through the bone.

Athena pressed the letter to her chest. She could not sit still. She would not. She paced the hard wooden floors trying to work out a plan. She needed to help. She knew that somehow, somewhere, someone, would be able to help. She could not let her sister raise four children on her own, and she would not allow her nieces and nephews to be raised as orphans. She grabbed her shawl and quickly ran out the door.

She stood outside the gates of the Presidential Palace in Athens for three days. Each morning, Athena returned with her modest, freshly washed dress, her black curls pinned back tightly and her shoes dusted from the gravel of Syntagma Square. She stood, clutching her letter, explaining herself to guards who rolled their eyes or sneered, but she did not leave.

On the fourth day, her persistence was rewarded. A young palace aide, kind eyed and curious, offered to take her name and her request. Hours later, she was led inside. The marble gleamed under her feet. Chandeliers hung like frozen fire from the ceiling. She was taken through a corridor where the scent of wax polish and old roses lingered. Then, the doors opened. Queen Frederika sat beneath a grand portrait of King Paul, regal in a navy dress and a pearl necklace that gleamed like a line of tears. She studied Athena with a calm and measured gaze. "You are the sister of the woman who wrote," she said in Greek. Her voice was firm but kind. "Speak."

Athena bowed her head respectfully, her fingers trembling around the letter. "Your Majesty," she began, voice thick with emotion. "My name is Athena Markopoulos. I came to Athens from Samos to work and to help my family survive. My sister, Aphrodite lives in Lekka. Her husband, Dionisios Yianopoulos was taken by the police. She has four children. They are starving and she is alone to care for them. He is not a criminal Your Majesty. He fought the Nazis. He is a good man." Frederika watched her quietly. "I do not ask for politics." Athena added. "I ask for mercy. I ask for children to see their father again. For a mother to have help. Please Your Majesty."

A heavy and sacred silence surrounded them. Then the Queen rose. She walked slowly to Athena, measuring her as if she were from another world. Her hands, gloved in white, reached out and gently touched Athena's shoulder. "You are brave," Queen Frederika said, her voice softer now. "You remind me of the women I met in the north during the war. They were fierce, faithful women, willing to carry the weight of a nation on their backs for the sake of their kin."

Athena blinked back tears.

"Saving one's family is not a crime. It is a noble blessing," the Queen continued. "And God does not forget such loyalty." She stepped back and nodded toward the aide. "Bring me the name Dionisios Yianopoulos of Lekka. We will look into his case. He shall be reviewed, and if there is no blood on his hands, no proof of crime, he will be released."

Athena fell to her knees, not out of duty, but out of sheer collapse and overwhelming gratitude. "Thank you. Thank you Your Majesty."

Frederika extended her hand, lifting Athena gently by the chin. "The country will heal one day. Women like you will make sure of it."

One week later, another letter arrived. Still not Father's blessing, but a letter from Aphrodite. Dionisios had been released. She said that he returned, thin and broken, but alive. Aphrodite said he kissed his children with quivering lips while she wept in his arms.

And in her modest room in Athens, Athena knelt in prayer and whispered thanks to the Queen, to courage, and to God. And she prayed that Father's blessing would soon arrive.

Father's letter arrived a few days later, heavy as a stone in her apron pocket. She stared at it for a long time before opening it, her hands shook so badly that she tore the paper slightly at the edges. Father's handwriting was rough and jagged. The words inside were even harsher.

Athena

"You will go to Canada."

"You will work."

"You will send for the family when you can."

"You are no use to us here, nor in Athens."

"Bring your brother and sisters to a better life Athena. That is your duty."

Father's letter was filled with orders wrapped in the selfish iron of survival. There was no blessing, no love, just commands. She swallowed the lump rising in her throat, trying to hold back the hot, bitter tears. She should not have expected anything more, not from him. Not after all he had done to them. Yet, some foolish, aching part of her had still hoped.

She found Dimitri that night by the low stone wall that bordered the outer edge of the city. The wind tugged at her hair, carrying the scent of lavender. He was waiting for her, a sweet smile on his face, a book tucked under one arm. When he saw Athena's face, the smile died. Without a word, he pulled her close. She buried her face against his chest, breathing in the worn linen of his shirt and the scent of him. "I have to go," She whispered, voice cracking.

"Where?" he asked, although she knew he already feared the answer.

"Canada," She said. "To work. To send for my family. To save them."

He stiffened, his hands tightening on her back. "And me?" he asked quietly. She barely heard him.

She lifted her head. The stars were bright above them, burning like promises. "I will come back for you," she said, the words tasting like blood. "I will find a way. I will bring you to me. Please, Dimitri. Wait for me."

Tears blurred his face. "But I love you," he said loudly, like a man carving words into stone.

"And I love you," she said, with all the strength she had left.

They clung to each other under indifferent stars, two tiny figures in the endless wreckage of a country still bleeding from too many wounds. When they finally pulled apart, she pressed something into his hand, a tiny woven cross, made from twigs. "Athena *mou*," (my Athena) he whispered, voice thick with grief. "Do what you must." His words were not those of encouragement, blessing or approval. His tone showed how torn he was.

"Whatever happens, I will send for you." She sobbed.

Dimitri nodded, unable to speak, and then he turned and walked away. Athena thought she would never have the strength to leave. Her feet felt heavy, almost buried deep in the ground. She stood there watching him for a long moment. She wanted to run towards him, to tell him how much she loved him, to stop him from leaving and to say that she would marry him. But she didn't. Instead, she slowly and selflessly began to walk the other way. Each step felt like betrayal, not only of him, but of herself. She was no longer the girl she had been before the war, before the hunger, before the fear and the tears. She had now become the one that needed to respect the choices and the duties that were were forced upon her.

The night air was sharp with the scent of ash. The gravel beneath her shoes scraped against the silence like a blade. She didn't look back. She could not, because if she saw him standing there, if she saw the way his shoulders curled inward like something inside him was broken, she would crumble. The city fell away behind her like a fading dream. Her chest burned. Her legs shook. She stumbled more than once on the uneven road, but she didn't stop. She couldn't. The future, whatever shape it might take, was demanding her sacrifice again, and Dimitri was the cost.

When she reached the bend in the road and the hills swallowed the last glimmer of Dimitri's silhouette, she collapsed behind a low stone wall. She buried her face into her arms, trying to muffle the raw, animal sounds that tore from inside her. She trembled with everything she had not said. The stars above watched coldly from their eternal distance as she cried for the love she was leaving behind, the life she might never have, the child she may never hold with him and the hands that would possibly not age alongside hers. The stars did not care that Dimitri was her anchor, they just watched aimlessly from afar while Athena walked away. That night, Athena slept on the cold floor, curled like a child, shivering beneath a thin sheet and the heavier weight of regret. She dreamed of his hands in hers, of dancing barefoot under the trees and of his voice whispering her name into the crook of her neck. The next morning, Athena awoke with salt on her cheeks and the dawn bleeding slowly into the horizon like an open wound.

The road to Athens had been long. She had traveled it alone. The ship to Canada would be longer, and she would, once again, be alone. But she knew that nothing, not time, nor distance would ever be longer than the night she turned away from Dimitri. Athena had once again, put others before her own heart and herself. She was a woman who chose duty over love. She was a woman who would spend the rest of her life wondering if she had lost the only real joy she had ever been given. And yet, somewhere in her heart, a quiet hope flickered. It was fragile but defiant. "Please, Dimitri… wait for me." She whispered as she pressed her hand to her chest. Then she walked towards a life that no longer felt like hers, alone and bruised.

The next days blurred into frantic preparation while her heart was still aching. She pressed her few belongings into a rough canvas bag. Father Marcus arranged for her passage, her paperwork and the letter of sponsorship that would let her enter the strange new world across the sea. She scrubbed the kitchen floors one last time while the soap stung her cracked hands. She folded the blanket on her cot as if laying down an old life, and then, on a gray morning heavy with mist, she boarded the great ship, the Nea Hellas bound for Canada.

Chapter 15: Across the Atlantic Aboard the Nea Hellas

The Nea Hellas loomed large and steel gray in the port of Piraeus, its deck bustling with porters and passengers, echoing with the clamor of shouted farewells. Its shiny hull gleamed against the sky while passengers clung to everything they could not carry, faces, homes, accents, and prayers. Athena stood on the dock, one small satchel in hand, the sea wind catching the edge of her coat and tugging at the kerchief tied neatly over her long black curls. This was the ship that would carry her across the Atlantic Ocean to Halifax, Canada, to a new world, a new life, and if God allowed it, to a future that might finally be her own. She tried to keep her chin up and her eyes dry as the ship's horn bellowed a deep, mournful farewell to Greece. She discreetly waved at the land she loved, and said goodbye to the land that had taken more than it had given.

As the ferry pulled away from the dock, she watched Athens shrink into a smudge on the horizon. Lekka's hills were nowhere to be seen. The tall and worn white buildings seemed to cling to the cliffs like barnacles. The trees bent in the wind like grieving women, and her heart ached with a hollow, wrenching pain Athena had never known before. She was leaving her blood, her history, her soul and her heart behind. All of these had been replaced by her carrying her family's hope. It weighed heavy as a stone on her chest, a life changing burden and a noble, selfless promise.

She held the simple gold cross Mother had pressed into her palm the night before she left Lekka and whispered her promise to the sea. "I will not fail you." Athena closed her eyes and saw Dimitri's face, his strong, stubborn jaw and his eyes that burned with belief. "Wait for me," She begged him silently across the widening water. "Wait for me, *agape mou.'my love.'*" The ferry shuddered forward. Athens began to disappear into the mist, and Athena turned her face to the unknown.

Athena stood at the foot of the gangway, fingers clutched tight around her travel papers and the letter from Father Marcus bearing the seal of the Holy Trinity's parish in Montreal. Dimitri's paper flowers and hearts were carefully folded and safely tucked into her worn prayer book. Behind her, the city lay still and heavy while the smell of diesel and seaweed lingered thick in the air. Somewhere beyond the ship's horn, church bells chimed a final benediction. She had promised herself that she would not cry, but she did.

Aboard the Nea Ellas, the scent of sea salt mixed with the stale aroma of boiled potatoes and kerosene, clung to the thick wool coats of the passengers. The ship groaned and creaked as it cut through the Atlantic, carrying hundreds of souls westward, away from the rubble of war and toward something called Canada. It was the unknown, an idea and a dream for many. It was more than a place, it was a future filled with foggy promises and imagined comforts. No one knew exactly what to expect at the end of this journey.

On the upper deck, where families huddled close, there were flashes of joy. Children pressed their noses against the salt streaked windows and ran along the narrow passageways, their laughter like a song over the steady hum of the engines. Mothers unpacked bread and olives wrapped in cloth, passing them around as if they were treasures. Fathers stood in small groups, sharing cigarettes and trading stories, their voices low but filled with a strange, swelling energy of excitement, disbelief and hope. The families that traveled together seemed lit from within. Their shared future glowed like a lantern between them, flickering and alive. They clung to one another during the rougher patches at sea, singing lullabies in the dimness of the lower bunks where whispered dreams of jobs, homes and new beginnings seemed to be the topic of conversation. For passengers like Athena, who stood alone, the crossing felt different. Her fingers gripped the railing tightly. Her face, though calm to a stranger's eye, was a map of sleepless nights and silent worry.

Athena stared out at the gray horizon, lips pressed shut, eyes full of questions she dared not ask aloud. There were others like her, young women traveling alone, widowed mothers with pale, silent children and men whose eyes moved constantly from their boots to the distant sky. They were the ones who had no one to lean on, no one to ease the tremble in their hands as the ship rolled beneath them. They were the ones who had said goodbye to everything and everyone, and now found themselves floating between two worlds, the past, which had abandoned them, and the future, which had yet to show its face. Athena's heart beat with a quiet thunder. She thought of her sisters, of Lekka's dry hills and of Mother's worn hands. She thought of Dimitri, his tender touch and shattered dreams. She thought of what she may have lost, and what she had to become. Her hope was there but it was buried deep beneath layers of fear, pain and fatigue.

The lower quarters were plain with steel bunks, lined side by side, stacked in threes like shelves in a pantry. The women slept on one side of the deck, the men on the other. There were no private cabins for girls like Athena, only thin woolen blankets and canvas curtains drawn for modesty. Her bunk was near the engine wall where its deep hum rattled her ribs. Each night as she tried to sleep, she heard the rhythmic groan of the ship's heart which felt almost human. To Athena, the groan seemed like it was someone mourning, suffering and carrying too much. Most passengers were like her, young men and women from war torn villages, families from Greek Islands or Europe's steadfast mainlands. Many passengers like Athena shared meals of dry bread, olives and fruit passed in cupped palms. Languages mingled in the dining hall like braids, Greek, Italian, Turkish, and many languages that Athena did not recognize.

Athena befriended a girl named Polixeni from Patras. She was bound for New York to join an uncle. They would sit near the edge of the ship, watching the sky lose its edges to the ocean. Polixeni spoke of dresses she would sew, of city lights and of American cinema. Athena listened and nodded, heart aching from the silence of Dimitri's absence. She tried to reassure herself that it would all mend when she would send for him. She dreamed of his warmth and his beautiful poetry. Each morning Athena opened her satchel to touch the photo of her siblings, seven smiling mouths and one empty space where she used to be. She admired the first gift Dimitri had made for her, the red paper flower he had hidden under the stairs. She smiled. *"I will bring you to me,"* she whispered. *"I will not stop until I do."*

The first few days on the ship were manageable. The seas were calm, the air fresh, and the novelty of being aboard such a great vessel was distracting enough to keep the knot of worry in her stomach from turning into something worse. By the fourth day, the Atlantic decided to show its temper. The sky darkened. The waves rolled like mountains. The ship pitched and groaned, and Athena, proud, dignified, respectful Athena, found herself gripping the railing on the deck. She retched up every bite of boiled rice and olives she had eaten the day before into the churning sea below. People tried to help. A kind British woman handed her a strange smelling biscuit. "It'll settle your stomach dear," the woman said with a soft smile. Athena, pale as a sheet and woozy, looked at her and groaned, *"Ti?"* (What?) The woman blinked, ran off and quickly returned with a cup of piping hot tea. Athena tried to respond, trying to gesture that *"Ti?"* meant (What?) in Greek, but another wave hit, and she was forced to lean over again, her kerchief flapping like a white flag of surrender.

A tall Frenchman offered her a small cup with a fizzy tablet dissolving in water. *"Pour l'estomac,"* (For the stomach) he said cheerfully. Athena looked at the cup, then at the man only to ask, *"Ti?"* (What?)

"Tea?" Another passenger blurted, "Oh, yes, tea's good for the stomach! I'll go get some!"

"No, no! *Ti?*" (What?) she mumbled, rolling her eyes slightly and grumbling in despair, her dignity trailing behind her like sea foam.

Athena spent the next few days mostly curled up below deck in her narrow blanket, with three other Greek women who were all as seasick as she was. The women bonded over their shared misery, groaning in unison and whispering prayers to Saint Nicholas, protector of seafarers, between sips of warm tea served to them by helpful passengers. They sometimes found the strength to smile at the mistaken question, *"Ti?"* (What?) that was followed by a serving of hot tea. Athena laughed, pledging to never, ever drink tea again.

The Nea Hellas was to make several stops along the way from Piraeus, Malta, Naples and finally Halifax where Athena would debark and continue her journey to Montreal by train. New York was to be the ship's final destination, but Athena barely registered any of it through the haze of nausea. When she did emerge on deck between storms and stomach flips, she marveled at the distant silhouettes of cities she would never truly see. She noticed the whitewashed walls climbing hills in Naples, fishing boats bobbing in calm island harbors and laundry flapping from balconies like flags of another world. At one point, she mustered enough strength to sit in the ship's small lounge, where a record player played faint, scratchy and warbled Greek melodies. A young boy approached with a deck of playing cards and said something in German. *"Ti?"* (What?) she asked again, managing a laugh between sips of ginger water as she knew that he too, would probably rush to bring her a cup of tea. He did, and Athena was finally able to truly laugh.

By the seventh day, the sea calmed completely. Athena could finally eat a full meal, and her color began to return. She ventured out more, walking the decks and meeting other passengers. Most were Greek, some Italian, and a few were Eastern European refugees fleeing the chaos of the postwar years. Stories were whispered in corridors at night, stories of families torn apart, of visas granted through churches and of dreams folded into letters sent back home. There was something oddly comforting in the shared hardship. The knowledge that everyone on board was chasing a better future, even if they didn't speak the same language, consoled her. On the tenth day, the Nea Hellas cut through thick morning fog and docked at Pier 21 in Halifax. Athena, dressed in her finest, a simple navy coat and black shoes, stepped off the ship. Her small crucifix stayed hidden beneath her blouse and her worn canvas bag was clutched tightly in one hand.

The customs officials were blunt and brisk, almost suspicious. They poked through her bag with sticks, rifling through her few belongings, a faded scarf, a battered prayer book, and the tiny wooden cross made from twigs.

"Name?"

"Athena Markopoulos."

"Occupation?"

"Domestic worker."

"Sponsor?"

"Father Marcus, Holy Trinity Parish, Montreal, Canada."

A grunt, a stamp, a wave of a hand, and just like that, she was in, no ceremony, no welcome, only the sharp slap of winter air against her face as she stepped onto the crowded docks. She looked around at the strange port. It was so different from Piraeus. The air was sharper, colder and the sky washed in a pale gray light. She was in Canada, a new world, a place where she hoped to earn enough to send for her family and Dimitri. This was a place where no one knew the name of her village, her father, or the weight she carried in her heart. As her shoes met the unfamiliar soil, Athena whispered under her breath, a quiet laugh escaping. *"Ti* voyage was that?"* (What voyage was that?) She breathed a sigh of relief, and was glad to finally be walking on land. She followed closely behind the women she knew were taking to the train to Montreal and breathed a long, deep breath of relief when they got in line to board the train.

Chapter 16: Across a Cold Land, a Familiar Face

The whistle of the train cried out like a lonely gull as Athena stood on the wooden platform at the Halifax station. Her canvas bag was heavier than she remembered. It wasn't the items she carried, it was the weight of purpose and of expectations pressed into her shoulders by years of poverty, obligation, and sacrifice.

The train station smelled of coal, damp wood, and salt. The Canadians rushed about speaking English, their accents sharp and clipped. Athena couldn't understand much, but she watched the rhythm of their lives unfold, fast and efficient, like the trains that thundered in and out of the station. Once aboard, the train rumbled through the vast Canadian landscape. Snow dusted the trees and rooftops, and the pine forests swept past the window like a dream. The vastness stunned her. Where were the olive groves, the crumbling stone homes and the orange trees? Everything here felt open and endless, like she had landed on another planet. For one full day and one night, she barely slept. Her bunk was narrow and the movement of the train jolted her awake with every stop.

Through the blur of cold windows and small towns, she felt an odd kind of wonder. She was no longer just the daughter of a broken mother, or the girl who had once been intrigued with a revolutionary in the mountains of Samos. She was not the girl who had fallen in love with a tender, loving and well read man in Athens. For the first time since leaving Lekka, she did not really know who she was anymore, and real fear pierced through her stomach.

When the train pulled into Montreal's *Gare Centrale* (Central Station) her breath caught in her chest. What had she done? She was a stranger here. She was a speck of dust in an indifferent, roaring world. No one knew her and no one cared. She knew that somewhere in the city of Montreal, Father Marcus waited. Somewhere, there was work to be done, money to be earned and letters to be sent home. Somewhere, there was a future she had not yet been able to imagine. She straightened her shoulders, took a breath that burned her lungs with coldness, and stepped forward into the crowd. She reminded herself that she was Athena of Lekka, daughter of stone and survival. She tried to encourage herself by thinking that she would not fail, not now and not ever, because she was Athena. She tried to convince herself that she was bound for something bigger and better. She then looked into the distance and noticed the swirling. It was not dust. It was snow.

Even here, oceans away, she saw a reminder of Father's curse. She breathed a profound sigh and proceeded to enter into her new world.

The cold in Montreal was different. It didn't roll in off the sea like in Samos. It dropped from the sky like strict discipline. It was much colder than Athena had imagined. The wind sliced through her thin shawl, biting into her skin as though the city itself were a ravenous living creature looking for warmth. The sky was a dull pewter color, the kind that felt like it would never quite brighten. A sharp wind whipped across the open port, pulling at the hems of coats and lifting ghost like steam from the trains. The city was a whirl of brick buildings, trolley bells, French and English signs that she could not read, and hurried footsteps that she could not hear.

Athena's boots slipped slightly on the icy wooden planks. She clutched her satchel tightly against her chest. Her breath came in shallow clouds. Everything felt enormous, the port buildings, the rail tracks, and the steel cranes stretched like metal giants into the sky. Foreign voices shouted in languages she did not understand. She turned slowly, eyes scanning the crowd of waiting strangers. People were wrapped in heavy coats. Some were holding bouquets and signs scrawled with names. Others, just like Athena, were craning their necks searching for something familiar, for someone who knew them.

A tall figure stood near the edge of the crowd. He stood straight, his hands folded behind his back, the silver cross on his chest glinting dully beneath the sky. His coat looked worn, but it was thick and dignified. His eyes swept the arriving passengers with calm intent. The moment he saw her, thin, tired and wrapped in a faded shawl, his face broke into a smile. It was Father Marcus. "Athena *mou*!" (my Athena) he called out, his voice like a balm over the chaos. "My girl!" he said, stepping forward as she crossed the icy pathway. Tears spilled down her cheeks. She ran to him, almost dropping her bag, and wrapped her arms around him. He smelled of incense and finally, something deep inside her relaxed for the first time in years. She tried to speak but no words came. Her lips trembled from cold and relief. Before she knew it, his arms were around her, warm and steady. He didn't say more, not right away. He simply held her, like a good father might, firm and safe. Hot, silent tears spilled quickly from her eyes. He pulled back slightly, looking her over. "You are finally here," he said gently. "Thanks be to God." Athena nodded, but she was still unable to speak.

The weight on her chest, that crushing loneliness that had ridden with her across the Atlantic, lifted slightly. She had made it to the other side of the world, and someone had been waiting for her. She thought of Dimitri, of his hands, his voice and his promises. She thought of the letter folded in her bag and Father's commands. *"You will go. You will work. You are no use to us here, nor in Athens. Bring your brother and sisters to a better life, Athena. That is your duty."* Those words clung to her like joeys cling to their mothers. Sadness filled her heart as she thought about the new life she had chosen, or rather, the life that had been chosen for her. Athena managed another nod. Her throat ached with all the words she wanted to say. *I'm here. I did it. I left everyone. I left Dimitri. I should have married him. I miss him. I'm scared,* but instead, she just clutched the edge of Father Marcus' coat and whispered, "I thought I might not recognize anyone here."

He chuckled. "How could you not recognize this beard?" He touched it, his eyes softening. "Come now. The cold won't wait. I have the parish car waiting." He took her satchel, light as it was, and placed his hand gently on her back guiding her through the crowd. "You'll stay at the rectory for now," he said. "Until we find you work with one of the families. There are good people here Athena. Greeks, just like us, very decent and God loving people. We will help you."

"You've grown into a beautiful woman, Athena." Father Marcus continued, holding her at arm's length to look at her. "Your mother would weep to see you now." Athena smiled through her tears. She had made it, and though her heart still ached for the land she had left, for Dimitri, and for her family across the sea, in that moment, she was grateful for not being alone. As they walked out of *Gare Centrale 'Central Station'*, she could see the skyline of Montreal, factories belching smoke, endless rows of buildings and church spires stabbing the sky like accusing fingers. Snow dusted the ground even though it was only October. She had never seen snow before. It looked like burnt ash but again, it reminded her of dust. Doom speared deeply in her gut. She feared that Father's curse had followed her across the Atlantic as she saw the snow swirling in the cold wind. She shivered, drawing her thin shawl tighter around her shoulders. Already, the cold was gnawing at her. She slipped her icy fingers under her coat while the cold pierced into her bones. Athena had stepped onto a new land, alone, but not defeated. She pulled her shawl a bit tighter, took a breath, and whispered the same words she had whispered on the day she left, "I will bring you here. All of you. I swear it." And then, like a soldier reporting for duty, Athena walked confidently into the snow, muttering, "I will not be weak. I cannot. They are all waiting for me to save them."

Her mind then escaped, once more, into the thought of the sun warmed fields of Lekka. She saw the golden light spilling over the stones and heard the soft buzz of bees in the olive groves. She took a deep breath and smelled the sharp tang of wood smoke in the evening air of Lekka. She felt Dimitri's warm and sure hands cupping her face. She thought of Mother, her bent back and her quiet endurance. Then she thought of her siblings, lying side by side like spoons in a drawer, teeth chattering in the cold and their bellies growling with hunger. She would be their shield, the armor to protect them from their fate. "I will not fail them." Athena whispered. She thought of Mother's last embrace and the strength she had when she clutched her close. "Stay strong," Mother had whispered. "For all of us."

Chapter 17: Life in a Foreign Land

Athena stood for a long time at the threshold of the tiny room Father Marcus had arranged for her, watching thick, heavy flakes of snow drift down from the colorless sky. The world had turned gray in an instant. The buildings surrounding her were tall and narrow, and through the heavy winter clouds, she could barely see the sky at all. Inside, the room was no more inviting. It was small, furnished only with a modest bed, a wooden table, and a single chair. A lone candle flickered on the windowsill, casting shadows that danced against the walls. Athena felt like a child again, retreating into a quiet corner of her mind, uncertain of what lay ahead.

Father Marcus had found her a job with a wealthy family. Mme. Lemoine, a French woman with a stern gaze and soft hands had hired her to clean and tend to the home. She spoke little, delivering commands in clipped, unfamiliar French, a language Athena was still struggling to understand. Athena listened carefully, memorizing every word and watching every gesture.

Mme. Lemoine had said that survival depended on obedience and precision. Athena tried to be as obedient and thorough as she possibly could. The work was relentless. She scrubbed kitchen floors until her knees burned. She dusted high shelves that seemed to stretch taller with each passing day, and washed laundry in a small, cold room that reeked of vinegar.

Each morning, Athena rose before the sun, and each night she collapsed into bed with bones aching and hands raw from the day's labor. When she closed her eyes, the cold seeped under the door, wrapping around her like an unwanted embrace, reminding her of how alone she truly was. It often felt like she was being swallowed whole by the darkness, but still, she worked because she had no other choice, and because she had made promises.

Warmth was a distant memory, but sometimes, just before dawn, in the stillness before the city stirred, Athena would close her eyes and let her thoughts drift back to Samos. She pictured the lemon trees swaying gently in the summer breeze, and she imagined the heat of the sun on her back as she worked the fields while Father slipped away to Persefoni's. She thought of the sweet taste of ripe figs and heard the laughter of her siblings echoing through the hills. In those quiet moments, she would dream of Dimitri, his strong arms wrapped around her while they stood together by the sea. Those moments never lasted because the cold and unyielding reality always returned.

Athena had never been one for indulgence, but living in Montreal seemed to sharpen the edges of her own restraint. Every cent Athena earned went into a small leather pouch, carefully hidden beneath the mattress in her room. She couldn't afford to waste a single coin. There was no room for indulgence, not when most of her wages were sent back to Lekka to support her family. Each time a letter arrived from home, she smiled at their words, but her smile was tinged with bitterness. She knew the cheerful updates were only a veneer, a softened version of the truth.

Her mother wrote that there was enough to feed the children and that the land had yielded a slightly better harvest, but Athena knew better. The letters were filled with forced optimism. Her family was trying to be brave for her, trying to convince her she had done the right thing by leaving. Still, each line twisted in her chest like a knife. There was never enough. There would never be enough for all of them. The money she sent home went to necessities like food, clothes and medicine. She rarely could afford to send anything extra, not even something small to lift their spirits. She certainly couldn't spare a single dime for herself. Her family depended on her. She was the one who was forced to make this choice and had left the island. Now, it was up to Athena to make that choice worthwhile. So when her eyes landed on an ice cream stand while sweet, rich and refreshing desserts glistened in the afternoon sun, she swallowed hard and walked right past it. Her mouth watered when she saw the chocolate dripping down the sides of the ice cream, and her stomach clenched at the thought of something cold and sweet, but she always refused. She couldn't yet allow herself that luxury. Every penny had its purpose.

Athena walked everywhere. She never took the bus, never wanting to waste money on transportation. The streets of Montreal remained foreign to her, filled with signs she couldn't read and voices she didn't always understand, but walking grounded her and she got used to it. Walking gave her the smallest sense of control in a city that often felt like it was swallowing her whole. With every step, she reminded herself that she was moving forward, toward something distant and undefined, perhaps hope? She expected that the sacrifices she was making, would eventually amount to something.

She worked from dawn until dusk, scrubbing, washing and dusting. The homes of Montreal's wealthy were nothing like the stone houses of Lekka. They were immaculate but cold and sterile. Their polished floors and gleaming kitchens held no warmth, and no sense of a life lived. The people she worked for were courteous but distant. They offered civility, not kindness. Occasionally, they extended a cup of tea, but Athena always declined. Since her voyage to Canada, she could no longer tolerate even the smell of tea. She also hesitated when they offered other snacks or drinks because she did not want to feel obliged. She was still a stranger in this land, and felt like in their eyes, she would perhaps always remain a stranger.

The hardest part of being in Canada came in the letters from Dimitri. At first, she had clung to them with the desperation of someone holding on to the last thread of a life she had once known. His words were a fragile bridge connecting her to her past and to the man she loved. They were her lifeline. His letters had been full of hope, and for a time, Athena convinced herself that she could endure anything. Montreal's cold, the isolation, and the exhaustion were bearable as long as she had Dimitri's love. The letters however, came less often, and started to show less and less hope. His words felt more like a sharp and sudden slap, and they sometimes cut deep. Athena's heart pounded, even before reading what he had written and his words swam in front of her eyes for days after receiving his letters.

"Athena, my love,

I think of you always, though it feels like you are a dream to me now. I have been waiting for you, but the days are hard. The mountain air gets colder. I fear that I may not be able to wait much longer. I thought that I would always be yours, no matter what happens. Time is showing me otherwise. I miss you dearly.

Please, Athena, be strong.

Find a way. Please find a way for us."

Chapter 18: Broken

Winter tightened its grip on Montreal. The snow fell heavier now, and the wind howled through the narrow alleys like a wolf searching for prey. Athena moved through it like a ghost, her footsteps steady but hollow. She still rose every morning before dawn to scrub marble floors of houses that didn't belong to her. She polished silver she'd never eat from and folded linens that smelled nothing like home. Her hands cracked from the cold water she used to wash linens and her knees bruised from hours of kneeling. But she didn't complain, she couldn't. She didn't cry anymore, she didn't have time to. All her energy was devoted to work.

On Sundays, she went to church where the familiar cadence of Greek prayers covered her soul like a balm. Father Marcus would nod at her from the altar, and sometimes, after mass, he would press a few coins into her palm, muttering something about God providing for the faithful. Athena didn't refuse his kindness, and she always added the money to the pouch beneath her mattress. Every coin still had a purpose.

When her sister Maritza's letter arrived, fragile and smudged with ink, it spoke of hunger, of danger, and of fear. Athena read it beneath her blanket by the candlelight, her breath seizing as she traced the words written in an unsteady hand. The burden of Lekka weighed on Maritza too. That night, Athena made a decision. She would bring Maritza first. She was suffering greatly, they all were. Whatever it took, she would bring her sisters and Pavlos to Canada, one at a time if need be. She would not allow them to disappear into that island's silence.

She began to ask questions, quietly and carefully. Other immigrants told her about the forms, the officials and the waiting lists. It would be hard. It would take time, but time was something Athena was used to giving. She had waited for love. Now, she would wait for her family to be united in Canada, and slowly, hope refilled her heart, not as a flame, but as a stubborn ember she refused to let die.

As the weeks passed, Athena resettled into the empty rhythm of her new life. The work grew more manageable, though it remained tiring. Mrs. Lemoine was kind in her own distant way, but it was clear she saw Athena as little more than a tool for the home's upkeep. She felt like a necessary presence rather than a person. The coldness of the city, both literal and emotional, crept into Athena's heart. Its steel edges slowly and silently chipped away at her courage. She missed the sun. She missed the warmth of the Aegean and the way her village came alive in the evenings, with conversations that carried into the breeze. She missed her family, especially the voices of her brother and sisters calling to one another through the hills of Lekka. With these thoughts engraved in her mind, she never stopped working, saving every coin, every penny, and every rare dollar, tucking it all carefully under her mattress. She would send it home, just as she had promised.

Each letter she wrote felt like a piece of herself was folded neatly into paper and sent across the sea. She told Mother everything about the city, about the biting cold, about the hours spent scrubbing floors and washing clothes. She told her that she was saving for the day she could bring them all to Canada, to a better life and to freedom.

Through it all, Athena never allowed herself to forget about Dimitri. The distance between them was unbearable, but she clung to her promises like burrs stuck to her clothes in the meadows of Lekka. She would bring him to her, she told herself. She would find a way to make a life for them here. She wanted him to be safe, to live freely and unafraid. She sent him letters every week, even when his replies became infrequent. Then, one cold evening in late November, a letter from Dimitri arrived. She opened the envelope slowly as though bracing for something she didn't want to read. His words struck like a stake to her heart.

"My dearest Athena,

This is the last letter I will write to you.

I've written and rewritten these words a hundred times, hoping the right ones might dull the edge of what I feel and what I must say. But there is no easy way to say goodbye to the woman you once dreamed of calling your wife.

You are everything I have ever admired in a person. You are strong beyond reason and kind beyond obligation. You carry the weight of the world on your back and still find a way to smile, even when that smile eats at your entire being. You are honorable, devout, and truly loyal. Perhaps that loyalty is what has broken us.

From the very beginning, I have known, though perhaps did not want to accept, that your heart belongs to your family first. I have waited for the day when I might come second only to God in your life. But as the days, weeks and months passed, your letters spoke only of your duties, of the money you send home, of the burden you carry for your mother, your siblings, and even your father. I came to understand something painful and permanent. There will never be enough space for us.

I do not ask that a woman forgets her family. God forbid. But I cannot live a life where I am forever in the shadow of your sacrifice. You chose to go to Canada, not for yourself, not for our future, but for theirs. And perhaps that was the right choice, but it was not our choice. It was his.

I fear your father's voice speaks louder in your mind than mine ever could in your heart. I have tried to understand. I told myself your duty is what makes you noble. But now I see it is also what makes you unreachable. You will give your life for others Athena, but never allow someone to give theirs for you. I wish I could be the man who waits forever, but I cannot. I am tired, and I want to build a life with someone who builds it with me, not around me.

You were, are, and always will be the woman I once loved beyond reason. And perhaps part of me will always love you, but this must be the end. May your new land be kinder than the old one. And may your heart, one day, belong to you again.

With sorrow and respect,

Dimitri"

Athena shook frantically. The paper crinkled under her tightening fingers. A fine tremor in her jaw betrayed what her rigid posture tried to suppress. She read the letter once, then again, and on the third time, the tears came hot and sudden. Not the delicate kind, not silent, these tears came with the choked sob of something ripped out from deep inside. She pressed the letter against her chest and doubled over on the edge of her small cot in the rectory room. Her shoulders shook silently in the dim light of a snowy Montreal afternoon. She closed her eyes, and for a fleeting moment, the world stood still. In the silence, she could almost hear Dimitri's voice in her ear. She felt his hand holding hers as they stood outside the cafe in Plaka, whispering promises of a future they had not yet seen.

This wasn't just heartbreak. It was fury. Not at Dimitri. She understood his pain. She had felt it too, but the fury was at Father and his blessing that never came. She clenched her fists thinking of the letter she had written to Father months before asking for guidance, and whether she could stay, to build a life in Athens and perhaps even marry a man she loved. She remembered his heartless reply, blunt, cold and commanding. Her nails dug deeper into the palm of her hands as she thought of his words. *"You will go. You will work. You are no use to us here, nor in Athens. That is your duty."* She had given everything, her youth, her heart and her future to obey a man who had given her only pain, fear and obligation. She had let Father decide that love would wait, that she could wait, and now, there was nothing left to wait for. She had spent years convincing herself she was doing the right thing. She had sacrificed her dreams, her hopes, even her future. She had given up everything she had ever wanted to honor a promise, a responsibility that had been placed upon her shoulders, and now Dimitri, the one person she had loved more than anything, was telling her it wasn't enough, that she wasn't enough. Faced with the bitter reality of losing Dimitri, Athena tried to escape into beautiful memories of Lekka's landscape, but her pain was too deep. She could not think of anything except her loss of Dimitri. She lay down and stared at the ceiling, tears trickling down her cheeks.

Chapter 19: Swollen Secrets

The rectory room was quiet. Athena lay awake holding Dimitri's letter to her chest. She traced the letters of the Greek alphabet in her mind like a prayer. Α, Β, Γ, Δ. She did what she always had done since she was eight years old. Tonight, all these years later, with snow falling softly against the Montreal windows, Athena thought about that bitter day, the day Father told her she was finished with school. Her face became blistering hot as fury took over her being. Athena's tears now began to dry rapidly.

She was only eight years old and just a girl, but like tonight with Dimitri's letter, something inside her hardened. It was then that she started to understand that in her world, some lives were simply valued more than others. Athena had taught herself to keep going long after Father declared that she had learned enough. Her sisters didn't know, neither did Pavlos. No one knew how many evenings Athena had spent using a hidden notebook stored secretly in the drawer beneath Mother's wedding night sheets.

It was hidden there, in the dim corner of the bedroom in Lekka, at the bottom of the cabinet. The old pine piece of furniture was swollen with years of secrets. Inside the last drawer, folded carefully, lay the wedding night sheet from her mother's bridal bed, pressed flat. The once white fabric, had yellowed with time, but it still bore the rust colored proof that the village demanded. This was the proof that a bride had entered her marriage untouched and pure. In Lekka, these sheets were displayed for all to see, flapping from balconies and clotheslines like holy relics. It didn't matter how the woman felt, what mattered was the stain and a man's pride. This was public evidence. Women were worth their blood, or they were worth nothing. In the village, a woman's worth was tied to a night and a stain. In some way, that folded object of virtue proved how well she obeyed the rules and how well she served.

Tucked just beneath Mother's wedding sheet, hidden like contraband, was Athena's notebook. Its pages were curled and soft at the edges, smudged with dirt from the fields and oil of her fingers. In it, she had copied out the Greek alphabet over and over again. The letters were tall and shaky at first, then they became steadier, like ants marching in rows. There were simple words, *γάτα,* (cat) *ψωμί,* (bread) *φως* (light) and then short sentences she remembered from school before she had to leave. *Η θάλασσα είναι μεγάλη.* (The ocean is vast) *Η μαμά αγαπά τα παιδιά της.* (Mother loves her children)

After Father declared that her mind had learned enough and now her hands needed to work the land, Athena had cried silently into her pillow. That same night, when the house slept and only the wind from the mountains kept watch, she slipped her notebook beneath the folded wedding sheet in the cabinet. She figured no one would ever look beneath it. No one dared touch the bottom drawer. It was the perfect hiding place.

Athena had refused to let her mind disappear. While she harvested vegetables, she rehearsed verb conjugations in her head. She hauled buckets of water, sounding out syllables under her breath. At night, when her siblings slept beside her, she would carefully lift the blood stained sheet, open her notebook, and continue her quiet rebellion in the shadows by the flicker of the oil lamp. The scrawled words in that notebook were the only part of her life that still felt like her own.

Years later, long after the fields, after immigration, after Montreal's harsh winters and lost dreams, she would still think of that drawer, of the sacred relic meant to prove, and the secret treasure hidden beneath it. She would sometimes smile, remembering that even then, she had known that the future was not written in blood, but in ink. Tonight, Athena could not smile even though she was proud that she had learned to teach herself.

Athena heard the cranking sound of the tram outside the church. She found the strength to stand. She slowly moved towards the doorway as if she were in a trance. Dimitri's letter was still tightly clenched in her hand. That's when she noticed it. Down in the corner near the radiator, behind a loose tile, walked an odd looking spider. She had never seen one like this. Its legs were impossibly long and glossy, its body, a slick and bulbous black. At first she froze as instinct tightened her shoulders. Then she leaned closer, her curiosity overriding her fear. The black widow moved with eerie precision. Her delicate legs tapped over the web she'd spun. Nearby, a smaller spider, her mate, twitched slightly, caught not only in the web, but in fate. Athena didn't look away. She couldn't. The female spider approached him slowly and deliberately. There was no hurry and no mercy. When she struck, it was silent. The male spasmed once and then went still. The black widow spider began to consume him without hesitation.

Athena pressed a hand to her mouth. Not out of fear, but out of the shock of understanding. She had seen this before. Not with spiders, but in the fields of Samos, in the narrow kitchen of their stone house and in the hard lines of Father's face. She had lived it. Father had devoured the strength of others to feed his own twisted sense of purpose. The black widow spider reminded her of Father, who sent his only son to school and his daughters to the fields. He had devoured his daughters' strengths to enrich his beliefs. Father drank and disappeared while Athena planted, harvested, and lifted sacks heavier than her own small frame. Father had consumed his own daughter, slowly, year by year, to serve his own purpose. It started in her childhood and continued with her learning. His consumption had reached the point where he destroyed Athena's future with the man she loved. Father said his choices were made out of necessity, not out of hate. Perhaps the black widow did not hate her mate either? She may have simply needed to feed for her own selfish purpose? Or maybe, like Father claimed, consuming her mate was essential for her family's very existence?

Athena stood there for a long moment, Dimitri's letter still in her hand, watching as the spider finished her meal and returned to the center of her web. Even now, across the ocean and all these years later, part of Athena still lived in that same web, woven tight by duty, silence, sacrifice, and curse. Unlike the spider's mate, Athena had not yet vanished. She decided right there, that her children, if ever she had any, would never be devoured for anyone else's sake. Athena would not pass this injustice down. She often wondered what life might have looked like if she'd stayed in school, if Father had allowed her just a few more years with books and teachers who spoke her name with kindness. Would she have written stories? Would she have become a teacher herself, or something even bolder, like a woman with her own name printed on an office door?

Even now across the oceans, she continued her quiet, defiant learning journey. She read grocery labels, in French and English. She studied the street signs like puzzles and underlined unfamiliar words in newspapers. Sometimes she whispered the words aloud, tasting them like a secret she wasn't supposed to know. Athena made another promise to herself. She decided that the ache she felt standing in the fields of Lekka holding a spade in her hand, her schoolbooks left behind, would never go further than tonight.

The storm inside her did not quiet. Athena slowly folded Dimitri's letter, smoothed its creases and slid it into the tin box under her bed with the others. She she should have known that her decision to put her family first, to honor her father's wishes would destroy everything. She stood still for a long while, the city's foreign sounds muffled beyond the window. Then, bitter, breathless, and still unconvinced, Athena whispered, *"You took this from me, but you won't take everything."* She sank to the floor of her tiny room, the cold of the boards seeping into her bones. She couldn't move and could not stop the tears. Knowing she was still tangled in Father's web, she buried her face in her hands. The weight of the world crashed down on her but she found the little strength left inside her to whimper into the stillness, *"Be strong, Athena. Be strong."*

As the days passed, Athena worked even harder. The letters from home filled with careful updates had grown bittersweet. Her mother still wrote, describing the harvest, the garden and the children's progress, but Athena could hear the strain behind the words. She knew they were struggling. They were trying to be brave for her, to keep up appearances. She could feel the unspoken fear in every line. She continued to grow angry, but she kept working. She kept saving. She couldn't stop now. Not when all her other dreams and promises had been shattered. In the quiet moments, alone with a scrub brush in hand and another floor beneath her, her thoughts drifted back to Dimitri, to what might have been, to the loukoumades they had shared under the stars, the walks along the sea, the love they once knew and the life she had abandoned. But it was too late now. All she had left was her obligation, and escalating resentment. The loss of Dimitri had carved a blusterous hurt inside her, one that no amount of work or sacrifice could fill.

Athena looked at the spider web and realized that for the moment, forgiveness was beyond her and forgetting was impossible. As days bled into weeks, her sorrow hardened even more. The faint, yet relentless voice inside her kept whispering, *God has a plan for you, Athena... something better.* as if trying to convince her. She clung to that phrase, desperate for it to mean something, but Athena continued to question if coming here was worthy of the pain and sacrifices.

Chapter 20: A Voice for the Heavens

Athena found Father Marcus in the rectory kitchen one late afternoon, just as the golden winter sun was setting. The wooden floor showed long shadows of golden streaks as the sun seeped through the windows. The scent of boiled coffee and wood polish hung in the air. He sat by the window with a book in hand, his glasses sliding down his nose. The brightness of the sunset made the lines on his face seem deeper in the light. She stood for a moment, uncertain, until he looked up and smiled gently.

"You've been quiet lately," he said.

Athena stepped in, holding the folded letter in her hand. "Can I sit?"

"Of course child." He gestured to the chair opposite his, setting his book aside. She didn't know how to begin. So she simply placed the letter on the table, pressing her palm to it like a seal.

"It's from Dimitri," she whispered. "He won't wait for me anymore."

Father Marcus looked at her with a kind of sadness that cut like a knife. He waited until her silence broke again.

"He says I will always choose my family over him. That I'm not capable of putting a husband first." She looked away quickly, trying to hide the tears. "Maybe he's right."

Father Marcus reached over and placed his large, warm hand over hers.

"Athena," he said, "there are moments when the world asks too much of us. But you gave what was asked with a pure heart. That is not a failing. That is a gift."

She looked down at her lap, fighting the shame. "I wanted to build a life with him, but I also wanted to save my family. I thought he'd understand."

Father Marcus's voice softened, yet it held its certainty like scripture. "Jesus gave His life to save those He loved. He did not wait for them to understand Him first. That is what true love does, it gives, not to be thanked, not to be rewarded, but because it must."

Athena's eyes teared again, but this time she did not hide them.

The priest continued, "Perhaps Dimitri is a good man, but not the one God intended for your journey. Sometimes, we must be emptied of what we want so that we can be filled with what we need. That is not loss. That is redirection."

She managed a tiny, bitter smile. "I feel like a fool."

"No," he said, shaking his head. "You are brave. You followed your conscience and your calling. You gave all that you could. You left your homeland, your language and your dreams to give, to help and to save your family. That is not foolishness, Athena. That is being noble, responsible and selfless." His words struck something deep within her, something aching to be understood. He sat back, eyes now gleaming with a lighter tone. "But even noble people must rest, and they must sing."

Athena furrowed her brow. "Sing?"

He chuckled. "Don't pretend you've forgotten. You had the most beautiful voice in Lekka. The entire island would quiet when you sang on Holy Friday. I've heard nothing like it in all my years."

Her cheeks flushed. "That was long ago."

"It is time to remember who you are," Father Marcus said. "The church choir is struggling. Too many women are working double shifts or raising children. You have no husband to care for, for now, and the Lord has given you this gift. Let your voice serve as your prayer. Let it carry you back to yourself."

Athena looked at him, unsure whether to laugh or cry. "You think it will help?"

"I think God gave you that voice for a reason," he said. "And if a man cannot love a woman for her voice, her courage, and her sense of duty, then he is not the man she was meant to build a life with."

Athena nodded. The pressure of grief was finally letting her breathe, and slowly, a small sense of release formed behind her ribs.

"Come this Sunday," he said, rising to refill their coffee cups. "The choir rehearses after liturgy. I suspect we'll need a soprano who sings like heaven remembers her."

She smiled through her tears. "Thank you, Father."

He handed her a cup. "No thanks needed child. Just sing."

That Sunday morning, the church of the Holy Trinity in the heart of the Greek quarter of Montreal stood cloaked in incense and pale light. The scent of beeswax candles mingled with the cold breath of winter that trailed in on the coats of parishioners, huddled under scarves and thick wool. The church was humble but beautiful with arched wooden ceilings, golden leaf icons watching from every corner, and sun slanting through the stained glass windows like a quiet blessing. Though the streets outside were gray and salted with slush, inside the sanctuary was warm and familiar. For Athena, it felt like home for the first time since she stepped off the Nea Hellas.

She stood near the back of the small choir loft, wrapped in a navy blue shawl, her knees trembling slightly, not from fear, but from the unfamiliar sensation of being seen and heard. She did not feel like a servant or a dutiful daughter, but as herself. The first hymn began softly. The other women around her raised their voices slowly, blending in familiar harmony. When Athena opened her mouth, something shifted. Her voice poured out, rich, pure and ethereal. It soared above the others not only in volume, but in clarity, like a bell ringing from the mountaintops of Samos itself. Her soprano was round and sweet, reverent, yet powerful. It wove through the domed ceiling, resonating against the cold stone and trembling the flames of the altar candles.

Heads in the pews turned. The rustle of jackets and whispered greetings faded into stunned silence. Elderly women made the sign of the cross in disbelief. Fathers stood straighter. Children stopped fidgeting. Even Father Marcus, lifting the gospel from the altar, paused as her voice filled the sacred space like a living prayer. Athena did not notice. She had left her body. Or perhaps, for the first time in years, she had entered it completely. While she sang, she did not think of the strangers whose floors she scrubbed or the calluses on her hands. She did not picture Father's face, or the ache of Dimitri's letter. She forgot about the spider and the cold sleepless nights she spent staring at the ceiling. She felt only the music, and tangled herself into the way each note lifted her from her burdens. The melody placed her gently into something greater. Her voice was not her own anymore. It was ancient. It was defiant, devoted and prayerful all at once. In that moment, Athena was not the girl from Lekka who had run from bruises and curses, nor the maid who counted every penny to feed mouths far across the sea. She felt like a vessel carrying beauty and relief across the house of prayer. When the final note of the hymn faded into the rafters, the silence was almost as moving as the sound itself. It was Father Marcus, his eyes wet behind his glasses, who finally broke the silence. He cleared his throat softly, "A voice sent from heaven," he said quietly, almost as if to himself.

After the liturgy, the parish buzzed like a stirred hive. Women clasped Athena's hands in theirs, praising her gift. Older men bowed their heads with solemn nods of approval. Young girls looked at her with awe, as though they had seen a new kind of woman, one who was holy and strong, humble and radiant. Athena, though grateful, did not bask in the recognition. She merely smiled, thanked them softly, and stayed near the icon of the Virgin Mary long after the others had left. There, in the flickering glow of candlelight, she lit a single taper and gently placed it in the golden candelabra. She did not light the candle for Dimitri, nor for Mother or her siblings, but for herself. For once, she prayed for the girl who had survived, for the woman who was rising, one note, one breath and one hymn at a time. As the shadows of the pews extended and the last echoes of her voice lingered in the wooden beams, Athena realized something quietly miraculous. For the first time since she left home, she was not simply surviving. She was becoming.

Chapter 21: The Woman She Became

Montreal's long winter waned, and by the time the church bells began to ring for Lent, Athena had become a radiant fixture in the Greek community. She was not loud or attention seeking, but Athena was impossible to overlook. People began to talk about her the way one speaks of a rare flower, growing unexpectedly in a snow covered garden. They spoke not just with admiration, but with awe. Athena had blossomed. Her beauty was the kind that didn't try. It didn't need decoration. She wore her long, black curls pulled back neatly and elegantly. At times her hair was twirled into a twist or a braided knot at the nape of her neck, revealing the gentle line of her jaw and the grace of her swan like neck. A few wayward curls would often escape to frame her olive skin like soft, black ribbons. It was not vanity that kept her hair styled, but discipline and a desire to present herself with care and dignity.

Her eyes were almond shaped, deep hazel, and expressive in a way that sparked and silenced a room when she looked up. She had eyes that carried old pain from Samos, with the quiet resilience of someone who had to transport more weight than anyone should before the age of twenty-two. Her eyes also carried warmth, tenderness and faith. When she smiled, which she often did, it was like the sun wriggling through the clouds. Her smile radiated with focus and its power lingered. Her waist was small, her frame modest but shapely, with a generous bosom that she dressed modestly in clean lines and simple fabrics. She wore mostly secondhand clothes, always ironed, always smelling faintly of lavender water or the soap she used to scrub them by hand in her small room. She wore nothing flashy, but still, she glowed. She walked with the kind of grace that came from from knowing exactly who she was, not from wealth or education, but from life's struggles. She was like an angel, not just for her physical beauty, but because of her presence. The way she carried her pain secretly showed others the portrait of a beautiful, strong, and caring young woman. The way she spoke gently to elders and knelt beside children as if they were treasures, made people admire her. Parishioners admired the way she offered help without waiting to be asked. They listened to the way her voice could lift a hymn into the heavens that had the power to make old men cry in church. She was modest, yet exceptionally radiant.

There were moments when Athena would catch men's eyes lingering on her. She understood why, but she never entertained them. She was polite, respectful and reserved. Some thought her cold, others thought her untouchable. In reality, Athena was simply devoted to her work, her family, and the vow she had made to build a better life for those she loved, everyone except Dimitri. She still thought of him often. There was no more room in her heart for distractions.

Athena still wrote letters home every week, slipping crisp Canadian dollars inside envelopes, along with small gifts like photographs, ribbons and sweets for her siblings. And yet, even with this love for her family, even with all she gave, Athena never looked worn down. She seemed to be the kind of woman hardship refined, rather than shattered. She made sure to look that way. One Sunday, as she descended the steps of Holy Trinity after Divine Liturgy bundled in her neatly belted coat and second hand leather gloves, she heard a woman whisper, "That girl, she's like a saint. A real lady from another time." Athena smiled gracefully knowing that while the world saw her as a beautiful, glowing and elegant, she still carried loneliness like a thread through her days. Singing, especially in the choir, continued to be the remedy for her pain. It was her prayer and her release. It was the only time she could transcend everything, her heartbreak, her exhaustion, the memory of Dimitri's final letter and the swirling of dust from Father's curse. When she sang, all of it seemed to fall away.

As spring bloomed across the city, lilacs blossomed along wrought iron fences. The St Laurence River sparkled under longer light and something within Athena also began to unfurl. Her sorrow still existed, but it no longer defined her. Her beauty was not just in how she looked, but in what she had survived and how she still moved through the world with grace. The girl who had once trembled in silence beside her siblings in the darkness of a village in Samos, had become a woman forged by sacrifice. She was radiant, not despite her past, but because of it. By the third year in Montreal, Athena had become something of a guardian angel to the new waves of Greek immigrants arriving by ship or train, worn from travel and heavy from the weight of displacement. Whether she met them in line at the Greek consulate, in the candle lit pews of Holy Trinity, or on the icy steps of a local bakery, Athena greeted them all with the same warm composure and a grin that soothed the most frayed nerves.

Her English was still touched with her island accent, and her French was limited to essential expressions and a welcoming smile. It was more than enough for those who spoke only Greek, and who looked to her as a bridge between their old lives and this foreign, wintry land. Athena helped young mothers fill out paperwork for residency. She took widowed elders to medical appointments, translating softly between doctor and patient, sometimes pulling out a notebook to show a phrase she'd written down and practiced that morning. She clipped job postings from newspapers and pinned them on the church bulletin board. She collected winter coats and boots to distribute to the newly arrived, many that still wore shoes better suited for Samos than the often snow covered Saint Laurent Boulevard. She did it all without seeking recognition. Her days were long, filled with cleaning jobs, errands, and volunteer work, but she never complained. Only sometimes, late at night, would she let herself think of the sacrifices she'd made, of the ice cream cones she never bought, of the money she sent home in thick envelopes to a father she feared and to siblings she missed more than she could bear.

Chapter 22: Two Sisters, Finally

Snow had already melted into the cracks of Park Avenue by the time Athena counted the last crumpled dollar and tucked it into the envelope marked *Canada, Εισιτήρια.* (Canada Tickets) Two hundred and ninety dollars for two tickets to Canada. She ran her thumb across the paper stained with the sweat of scrubbing other people's floors. It had taken over a year, a whole calendar's worth of aching feet and trembling limbs, of forgoing meals, pinching pennies, and hoping that maybe one of the women whose homes she cleaned would offer her a slice of cake, a bit of feta or a single boiled egg. Athena had done it. She had saved enough for two ship tickets on the Nea Hellas, each costing one hundred and forty-five dollars. She sealed the envelope and sent it to Lekka. Then she waited.

Athena cleaned many homes every week, several homes each day, six days a week. She walked from Papineau to Outremont, from Côte-des-Neiges to Mile End to make sure to save every penny she could. Even when her shoes wore thin and her legs burned, a bus ride was five cents she couldn't spare. She would rise before the sun, tie her black hair back tightly so she looked neat and professional and pinched her cheeks for color before entering each house. In four hours, each house sparkled without a speck of dust left behind. She moved quickly but with care. The silver was polished impeccably. The tiles gleamed brightly and the sheets were clean, crisp and fragrant. She folded towels like pressed flowers.

Her clients were the wealthy wives of men, some from the Greek Orthodox church. They were women who had never scrubbed a floor or boiled their own coffee. They called her "our sweet Athena" and whispered to one another that she was the best domestic worker in all of Montreal. Some pitied her and some were proud of her. A few invited her to sit for a coffee or to nibble on leftovers. Athena never asked, but she always said thank you. On Sundays, she rested, not in the way others might rest, lounging, napping or reading a book. No, Athena dressed in her best and went to church to sing. Her voice floated over the congregation and filled the sanctuary with something warm and holy. Those who knew of her work week couldn't understand how she still had breath left to sing, but that was when Athena felt most alive.

She was polishing brass handles when she opened it. The cloth fell to the floor. Father still monitored everything. The envelope had been opened and resealed, as it always was. The handwriting was Mother's, inside, a small note, *"Your father has chosen to send Maritza and Christina first. They are still young, and he says they will learn the language quickly. He says they must help you, so you can bring the others too."* Athena pressed the letter to her chest and cried silently in the kitchen of a home on St. Urbain. Maritza and Christina, her sisters were finally coming.

Athena's heart swelled with joy and a slight disappointment, not because it wasn't someone else, but because she hadn't gotten to choose. She was glad Maritza was chosen because her last letter had shown her suffering. She imagined both their faces, thin, tired and brave, stepping onto the ship, not knowing what would greet them. She sighed. Father still pulled the strings from across the sea, but her disappointment quickly turned to relief. Two of her sisters were finally coming.

The Nea Hellas would arrive in Halifax soon, and from there, Maritza and Christina would take the long train ride to Montreal where Athena would meet them at *Gare Centrale, 'Central Station'*. She bought them each a woolen coat and two pairs of socks. She picked out a small, second hand purse for Christina, and a knitted scarf for Maritza. The room she rented on Jeanne Mance Street was barely big enough for one, but she arranged her blankets and mattress to make room for two more bodies. Luckily, it was bigger than the rectory room. It would be tight, but they would be warm, safe and together, at last. That night, she sang at choir practice like a woman on fire. Not even the aching in her back, nor the calluses on her hands could dampen her voice. She sang for her sisters. She sang for the long road they had ahead, and she sang for the belief that one day, she would bring them all to Canada.

She had risen at four in the morning. She hadn't really slept. Every hour of the night before was restless, her thoughts circling around two small faces she hadn't seen in years, blurry with the passage of time. She wore the green woolen coat she saved for church. It was crisply pressed and tidy. She put on the small black scarf Father Marcus had gifted her, neatly tucked at her neck. Her boots were scuffed but clean. She wanted to look proud and capable, like a woman her sisters could trust.

The train station was a cavern of iron and glass, its domed ceilings echoing with the hollow clang of hurried footsteps and the low grumble of incoming trains. Athena stood near platform 7, butterflies in her stomach, twisting the fabric of her coat between her fingers. Her eyes darted between arrivals and the clock overhead. Snow flurried through the high windows, melting into slush on the stone floor, but Athena could not feel the cold. Her skin burned from excitement. The train from Halifax groaned into the *Gare Centrale 'Central Station'*, dragging car after car past her. Athena's chest tightened. People poured onto the platform, men with suitcases, women clutching children and families reuniting in tearful hugs. Then, two girls appeared in the distance. They seemed tiny beside the sea of strangers, wide eyed and pale from the long journey. They were wrapped in big coats that swallowed their fragile frames. Maritza wore the pin Athena had sent and Christina clutched her little purse like a sacred treasure. Athena's legs moved before her mind caught up. Her voice broke into a high pitched, aching cry, *"Κορίτσια μου!"* (My girls) Christina and Maritza turned to follow the voice. Their eyes lit up like wildfire. *"Αθηνά!"* (Athena)

They collided into her, threw their arms around her waist and pressed their heads against her chest. Athena sank to her knees, holding them close. She could smell sea salt, ship metal and the scent of foreign food in their clothes. She kissed their cheeks again and again. She murmured their names, *"Christina! Maritza!"*, as if to confirm they were real and alive in her arms. Maritza cried softly, her face buried in Athena's coat. Christina held her tighter than a girl her age should have strength for. "I missed you," she whispered in Greek.

"I missed you too," Athena said, choking back tears. "So much."

People passed, glancing at the three girls huddled on the platform floor, but Athena didn't care. In that moment, the noise of the station, the weight of her exhaustion and the loneliness disappeared. She was no longer alone in the new world.

They walked back to the room on Jeanne Mance, giggling and laughing, arms linked tightly. Athena guided them across snowy sidewalks and beneath the skeletal arms of leafless trees. She carried their small bags, heavy with the scent of Lekka and the weight of Father's instructions. The girls looked around at the tall buildings, their necks craning to follow the streetcars. Maritza asked if all the roads in Canada were this wide. Christina was quiet, her fingers constantly gripping Athena's hand. Inside the tiny room, Athena had made their bed warm with extra blankets. She had boiled water for chamomile tea and had laid out bread with butter and cheese. They sat together on the mattress, the girls blinking sleepily but smiling, eyes full of wonder and joy.

"Tomorrow," Athena said, brushing Christina's hair, "we go to church. We will light a candle to thank God you've arrived safely. And then…" she hesitated, "then we begin."

"Begin what?" Maritza asked.

"Bringing the others." She didn't say it with bitterness. She said it with fire.

Later that night, when the girls were asleep beside her, Athena stared at the ceiling and allowed herself to smile. They were curled into her sides like they used to be when they were small. "Two down. Six to go." Athena whispered into the darkness.

Chapter 23: Three Sisters, One Dream

On their first Sunday in Montreal, Athena dressed Maritza and Christina in secondhand laced dresses she had hemmed by hand late into the night. They wore thick stockings and each wore one of Athena's scarves, ends tucked into their coat. Their boots were a little big, but lined with paper to keep their feet warm. Snow had fallen overnight, blanketing the streets in soft, white silence. The girls pressed their noses to the window of Athena's small apartment, their breath fogging the glass.

"Χιόνι!" (Snow) Christina whispered.

"όπως η ζάχαρη!" (Like sugar) Maritza said.

Athena buttoned her coat and smiled gently. "Come."

Outside, the snow crunched underfoot as they walked. Christina's mittens were mismatched. Maritza slipped on patches of ice, clinging to Athena's arm and giggling. It had been so long since Athena had heard her sisters laugh. She let herself laugh too. Her heart was lighter than it had been in months. The girls admired the Holy Trinity Greek Orthodox Church. It stood like a stone anchor on busy Sherbrooke Street. Its bell tower stood tall and proud, a beacon for the scattered Greek souls seeking comfort in this faraway land. Inside, incense hung in the air like the memory of centuries of sorrow and salvation. The pews were filled with the warm colors of friendly faces, old women in black headscarves, men with working hands and children fidgeting restlessly. The liturgy echoed through the domed ceiling, sung in Greek, unchanged for a thousand years. The girls sat beside Athena in awe. Christina whispered, "It sounds like home. It's wonderful!"

When Athena rose to join the choir, her sisters' eyes were wide and shining. They followed her in admiration. Father Marcus smiled when she stepped into place. "Your sisters?" he whispered. Athena nodded. He placed a gentle hand on her shoulder. "Sing like they've never heard you sing before." The choir began. Her voice rose, clear and rich, like warm syrup poured over snow. It filled the church, dipping and soaring like wings over the congregation. The old women whispered quietly. Children turned to look. Even Father Marcus paused at the altar to listen. Maritza and Christina sat in stunned silence. It was not just a song. It was home. It was everything Athena had kept locked inside, her sacrifice, her sorrow and her love. It poured out of her, into the rafters and down over her sisters like a blessing. For the first time since she left Samos, Athena felt whole.

After the service, parishioners came to greet them. *"Τα κορίτσια σου, Αθηνά;"* (Your girls Athena) So beautiful!" They offered fresh koulourakia, cocoa, and warm embraces. The girls beamed. Athena stood proud but humble, accepting compliments with bowed eyes and a grateful heart. Father Marcus found her in the hall. "You reminded us today of what heaven sounds like," he said softly. She blushed, and her heart warmed.

The girls tugged at her sleeve. "Can we come again next Sunday?" Athena smiled. "Every Sunday. This is our new home and we must remain close to God." As they stepped outside into the falling snow, the church bells rang above them. Athena felt something she hadn't felt in a long time. She finally felt peace.

It didn't take long for Maritza and Christina to fall into the rhythm of Montreal's harsh winters and hardworking days. Athena had carved out a life with grit, and now, with her sisters beside her, they moved like eagles, free, smooth, and strong. They shared Athena's small room in the triplex on Jeanne Mance Street. Christina slept near the radiator and hummed in her sleep. Maritza always rose first, brushing her long black curls in the mirror. Every morning in the kitchen, they huddled over Greek coffee and bread before heading out to work.

Christina found work mending linens for a hotel on Park Avenue. She was quiet and observant. She had a gentleness to her that made her trusted, even among strangers, She was the first to pick up enough French to help her coworkers communicate. She had a way of fading into the background, but she saw everything. Maritza was different. She was loud, quick to laugh, and she had a gritty sense of humor. She brought levity into every room she entered. Her eyes crinkled tight when she laughed. They were small, lively and sparkling with mischief. Her laugh rolled out with bell like bursts that made even the sternest person smile. She was not tall, but she was voluptuous. Her hips swayed elegantly when she walked. She drew attention without meaning to and she enjoyed it. She often left her long, curly, jet black hair sway loose, like a silky curtain down her back.

Christina would often scold her, "Collect yourself, Maritza! What would *Baba* say?" Maritza would wink and toss her hair. "If *Baba* had a laugh like mine, maybe he wouldn't have been so angry all the time." Still, Maritza was not just laughter and eye appeal. She was suspicious of strangers and distrusting of compliments. She crossed her heart every time she saw a black cat or spilled salt. She hung a blue glass *mati,* (a baby blue glass eye) above their doorway. She was convinced that too many admiring glances could ruin everything they'd worked for by casting the evil eye.

Despite her playfulness, her roots ran deep into old superstitions. Her instincts were sharp but often unfounded.

Together, the three sisters cleaned homes, laundered, scrubbed, folded, mended, and saved. Athena taught them to walk from one job to another, no trams, no busses, and no spending. They pooled their money together to pay for utilities and food. They packed olives, boiled eggs, and bread in wax paper. When women offered leftovers from their kitchen tables, the girls never refused, though Athena still blushed with pride. They pooled their money in a mason jar hidden beneath a floorboard. Every week, they added to it.

Their first goal was for 7 more tickets. Then, they would need tickets for Eleni's husband Christos and their daughter Amalia, and finally, Aphrodite's husband Dionisios and their four children, Anthoula, Kaliopi, Vassilis and Voula. The list seemed endless. It was an almost impossible feat, but Athena kept a ledger by her bedside. She marked down every dollar, calculating and recalculating, months in advance. "We'll bring them all," she promised one snowy night as the three huddled beneath the same blanket. "No one will be left behind."

Christina clutched her rosary. "Even Pavlos? Father will never let him go."

Athena hesitated, "Yes, Even Pavlos." she huffed. "Mother, and Father, Aphrodite's family and Eleni's family too."

The hours were long and the work unforgiving. Rich women clucked their tongues if the silver wasn't gleaming and frowned if the laundry smelled too much of vinegar. Maritza almost left a job when a woman slapped her hand and called her "the little peasant girl with hips like a mule." But she didn't leave. They had a purpose and jobs were not easy to come by. They cried sometimes and sang often, but they never gave up, not even when disrespected by their employers. The Greek community had noticed them too. The girl with the angelic voice and the two sisters who matched her beauty and grit. They began to call them *"ta korítsia apó ti Sámos"* (the girls from Samos) and all the while, the jar under the floorboard grew heavier.

They couldn't stay in Athena's small room anymore. The tiny room on Jeanne Mance did not have enough space for another mattress. They were tired. All three of them sleeping horizontally on one mattress was not allowing them to rest well enough. Besides, they had now collected enough money for another ticket from Greece. They would soon be four, so they needed to find another place to live.

The apartment on Cartier Street was nothing special, but to Athena, Christina, and Maritza, it was a palace. It had two small bedrooms, a narrow galley kitchen with creaky cupboards, and a bathroom that moaned every time the taps were turned. The floors tilted slightly toward the center, so if a marble dropped, it would roll from the front door to the back window without much effort. Still, the girls scrubbed every inch until it gleamed. They stitched lace curtains and pinned embroidered doilies to every surface. The scent of oregano, lemon, and soap hung in the air. From the tiny balcony, they could just see the curve of the Jacques Cartier Bridge stretching like steel lace across the sky. On the clearest days, the silhouette of Saint Helen's Island, the former World War II prisoner of war camp #47, lay green and hazy beyond the river. That sight stirred something in Athena. The island had no olive trees, no whitewashed walls, but somehow, it reminded her of home. Saint Helen's Island held the history of a painful strip of land, suspended between two worlds, just like Samos.

On Sundays, after church, the sisters would walk down Cartier, past the butcher shop and the grocer who spoke only French. They went toward the bridge, their shoes clipping on the pavement, their scarves tight over their hair. The wind off the river tugged at their skirts, but they pressed on, arms looped together. They'd cross the bridge laughing and humming old folk songs and walked among the pines and lawns of Saint Helen's Island imagining they were somewhere in Samos. Sometimes, Maritza would dance between the trees like a nymph, her laugh echoing through the air. People would stop and stare at the dark haired girls speaking Greek, arm in arm, with eyes full of memory and purpose.

But Montreal was not always kind. The names started quietly, sharp like needles in whispers as they passed. "*Maudit Grecques. Y parlent même pas français, ostie..*" (Damn Greeks. They don't even speak French) One day when Maritza tried to ask for change in broken French, a woman rolled her eyes and hissed, "Go back to your country." Another time, outside the laundromat, a group of boys pointed to the girls' feet and barked like dogs. The girls didn't laugh on those days. Maritza's fire would flicker low, and Christina would pull her handkerchief tighter. Athena, ever the shield, would gather them close and whisper, "Let them speak. They don't know who we are."

Still, not everyone turned away from the girls. An old Québécoise neighbor, Mme. Boudreault, once found them in the stairwell. Athena was clutching a ripped grocery bag and crying softly after a man had cursed, pushing past her on Saint Laurent Boulevard. When she told Mme. Boudreault, the neighbor answered with a quiet kindness, "Don't let people like that teach you how to speak to yourself." From that day forward, Mme. Boudreault would leave a pot of soup at their door on cold evenings. Another neighbor, Mr. Côté, a widower who lived downstairs, offered them his old Victrola record player and taught Athena a few phrases in French. He was married to a Polish woman, and said he had a soft spot for "strong women with accents and hearts like lions."

There were stares, and sometimes still name calling, but there were also defenders. Some people saw their fatigued eyes, tired hands, and the way they kept their dignity like a pearl in the pocket. Those smiled kindly. At night, when they returned home from work, the girls lit a candle under the Virgin Mary icon they prayed to. They made Greek coffee, and sat on the floor of their crooked kitchen. They continued dreaming of the day their whole family would be there. They aspired to better days together. The bridge, the island across it, the city, even the hurt was all part of the crossing.

And then came Aristotelis.

Chapter 24: A New Face, New Feelings

It was a Sunday evening, May 21ˢᵗ, when she met him. The world was on the cusp of spring, the trees blooming despite the slight chill still lingering in the air. A Greek friend, Kostadina, was hosting a name day gathering in her small flat on St Dominique Street. A long table groaned under platters of spanakopita, loukaniko, olives, and baklava. The room smelled of retsina and oregano. Laughter echoed off the cracked plaster walls, and someone had started playing the bouzouki he had brought onto the ship from Kastoria. Athena had almost not gone. She rarely attended parties but Kostadina had insisted, and Father Marcus had nudged her gently to "Be among people your age, my child. You deserve some joy."

When Aristotelis entered, late and laughing, everything around him seemed to part like a curtain. He was tall and lean but broad shouldered, with black, wavy, slicked back hair. His upper lip was adorned by a neatly trimmed mustache that hid a radiant crooked smile. His eyes were golden brown like dried figs in sunlight. He scanned the room with a mix of confidence and detachment until his eyes landed on Athena. After their introductions Aristotelis asked with a slanted grin, "From Lekka?" His voice was smooth and tinged with the sing song lilt of the Ionian Islands. "And you came all the way to Montreal to sing like a nightingale and save the world?"

She laughed, a quiet, genuine laugh that surprised even her. "And you?" she returned, lifting an eyebrow. "From Kefalonia? You came here to flirt and steal pastries from party tables?" They both laughed, enjoying the playful teasing. They stood near the balcony, away from the noise, where the fresh breeze squeezed through a cracked window. They spoke for hours, their words slow at first, then spilling freely. They spoke about the sea, about how the stars looked different in Montreal than they did over their islands. They talked about how the ache of missing home never really left. They were both islanders and both carried the weight of families left behind. Aristotelis spoke of his dream to one day own a chain of restaurants and bring his sister and brothers to Canada. He was proud, charming, and amusingly cynical.

Athena was cautious. Where Dimitri had burned with ideology and passion, Aristotelis sparkled with charm and mischief. He made her laugh. He teased her gently when she mispronounced an English word. He said her seriousness was beautiful and that her eyes were the color of the Ionian Sea after rain. He said that her voice, when she sang, could make him believe in God again. They spoke for hours. Athena quickly realized that he was different in a way that unsettled her, but she was intrigued by him. Aristotelis lived for the moment. He spent his wages on good wine and new shoes. He joked that life was short and that worrying about tomorrow never made today sweeter. Athena, whose every coin was saved, whose every step was planned, found this freedom both enticing and dangerous.

They saw each other every Sunday. He stood near the back of the church, hands behind his back and his shoulders slightly hunched. For a time, Athena noticed how Aristotelis bowed his head when the priest raised the chalice. His suit was clean, and he sang *Kyrie Eleison,* (Lord have mercy) with a voice that did not waver. They had conversations in the echo of the church and a few stolen moments in the churchyard while the others laughed and kissed cheeks to say goodbye. Aristotelis was often careful with his words, as if afraid to give away too much.

Montreal's Greek community had many ghosts, men who had slipped through borders and oceans to find work and refuge. Aristotelis had come like that, on a cargo ship from Italy, stowed between crates of marble and machine parts, breathing in salt and rust for days until the ship docked. Then, he simply walked off the ship, no passport, no papers and just vanished into the city.

"I won't be here much longer," he said.

"Why?" she asked.

He looked at her with a quiet smile. "Because I'm not supposed to be here." And then it spilled out. He told Athena how he had escaped Greece during the civil war, how he had made his way through Europe, sleeping in barns, hitching rides on trucks, bribing his way into the port at Genoa, how the ship's captains sometimes looked the other way for a few drachmas and how he landed in Montreal like a shadow.

"But why not go back now?" she asked.

He shook his head. "There's nothing to go back to. No work, no peace, and no place for men like me."

Athena's heart ached at his words, but there was something else beneath the surface, something less noble. Aristotelis was charming, but she had already seen that he didn't carry burdens, he dropped them. He lived for himself and when he looked at her, it seemed like it wasn't only with longing, but with calculation. Still, she kept talking to him because he impressed her.

Aristotelis liked to watch her. She could feel it when she served at the church kitchen, when she walked home with her sisters and when she bowed her head in prayer. Athena caught him staring often. There was hunger in his gaze, not just for her, but for the life she represented. A woman with roots, with purpose, with family and with papers.

"You work too hard," he told her one afternoon, as they sat in the empty pews after liturgy.

"I work because I must," she replied. "You don't?"

"I work to survive and to grow. That's not the same."

She turned toward him. "It should be."

There was a long silence between them filled only by the distant toll of bells. He reached for her hand, and for a moment she didn't pull away. His touch was warm, but the warmth didn't spread. It stayed there, confined. There was something about Aristotelis, a rebellious kind of freedom and a recklessness she had never allowed herself to feel. She had always carried the weight of others. He had none of that, and yet he wanted her, the rooted woman, the good woman, the one who never let herself break. As spring bled into summer, the whispers started, about a raid, about papers and about someone being picked up near the docks. Aristotelis began to vanish again. One week he was at church, the next, he was not. She once saw him outside the bakery on Roy Street. It was at dusk. He looked thinner and older. The charm in his eyes was dimmed by fatigue. "I think it's only a matter of time," he said softly. "before they find me."

Athena nodded. She felt no tears, only a strange, dull ache in her chest. "Where will you go?"

He smiled. "Wherever the next ship takes me."

For a brief moment, she longed to drift away too.

"Why do you always put others first?" he asked her once after she'd skipped dinner to help an elderly man from the church find his missing immigration papers. "Don't you ever want something just for you?" She didn't know how to answer because she did, but she felt guilty about it. She wanted joy, a life of her own, a hand to hold and a home filled with laughter instead of violence. She had been taught by survival, by sacrifice and by her mother's bruised face. Her life had taught her that wanting too much was dangerous.

Aristotelis was patient. He didn't push. He invited her on long walks through Mount Royal Park where he would point to houses on Cote St. Catherine Street in Outremont and say, "One day, that will be ours." He brought her flowers, tiny daisies plucked from sidewalk cracks. He spoke to her in slow French, practicing together under the moonlight.

Athena remained grounded. She felt that her life could not yet be a love story. She was still building something, a life made of honor and duty. She was structuring a life built with hope and struggle not romance and recreation. And yet, for the first time in years, she allowed herself a quiet question, *What if, one day, love could be a part of that too?*

And often, she thought of Aristotelis.

Chapter 25: Four Candles in the Cold

The envelope from Lekka was smudged with fingerprints and sealed tight with Father's rigid script pressed across the back. Athena opened it slowly and hesitantly, not knowing what she would read. Inside was the news they did not expect, Father had finally used the money they had saved to purchase a ticket for Pavlos. Much to everyone's surprise, Father had decided that Pavlos should come next to protect his unwed sisters. Pavlos, Father's pride, his only son, his legacy was on his way to Canada. Athena looked across the table at Christina and Maritza, their eyes wide with a mix of surprise, joy, and apprehension. It wasn't just that they would soon be reunited with their brother, but they all knew what his arrival meant.

Pavlos wasn't coming to start a new life on equal footing. He was coming as the man of the family. The one sent to *"watch over"* his sisters. The one tasked by Father to *"make sure the girls behave,"* to keep them *"respectable,"* to remind them of the values they had been raised with in Lekka. They knew Father's intention, but they also knew that their only brother was more than welcome to join them in Canada. He would help them, and he would also make it easier to communicate with Father. Pavlos was the only one that Father listened to. They knew that with his help, their whole family would be in Montreal much sooner.

When Pavlos stepped off the train from Halifax, he wore a coat that was much too short at the arms. He clutched a canvas bag that smelled of damp wool. His shoulders were broader than when they'd last seen him, but his face still carried the softness of the boy who used to hide in the mountains with his sisters, whispering stories of faraway places. Athena wept as she embraced him, her head pressing to his chest. "You're here," she said through her tears. "You made it." He didn't say much that first night. He looked around their modest apartment on Cartier Street, nodded his approval of how well organized and how clean it was. He commented on the meals, "You cook like *Mama*." Then, with a low voice, he added, "*Baba* sends his regards. He expects you to keep honoring the family name." The girls exchanged glances but said nothing. They had known it would be this way. Still, there was joy in hearing his laugh again, in watching him tease Maritza. With Christina, he argued about old songs, and he fixed the loose doorknob on their bedroom door as though it were a sacred duty.

Pavlos had been raised with the weight of legacy and burden, but he loved his sisters deeply. That had not changed.

Weeks passed and the apartment swelled with life and shared responsibility. With four of them now working, Athena cleaning, Christina and Maritza taking shifts in hotels and Pavlos learning the trade of butchering from a fellow Greek immigrant, the savings began to grow again.

One night, after lighting a candle for Saint Nicholas, Athena counted out their earnings. She pushed the final few dollars into the tin box they kept under the floorboard. "It's enough," she whispered. "Another ticket." They celebrated together that night, laughing and singing folk songs, proud of their efforts, and in the distance, the sound of the Jacques Cartier Bridge hummed like a lullaby. The next envelope from Lekka came faster than expected. Once again, Father had made the decision. This time, it was Anna, the baby was coming to Canada. Anna was fifteen years old. "She's old enough to help," he had written. "The house is too full. Food is scarce again." Athena read the words over and over. She couldn't imagine Anna, with her long, thick braids and childhood innocence, leaving the hills and orange groves behind, but there was no choice. Father had chosen. He always chose.

On a cold afternoon in March, they met the next train at *Gare Centrale* (Central Station). Anna descended the ramp like a ghost of their past, her frame swallowed in a thick black coat with a white comb poking out of her knapsack. She looked up, blinking against the snow, and then, she ran. Athena opened her arms, and in that moment, everything disappeared, the years of aching feet, the humiliation, the work and the distance. Anna was in her arms. Her baby sister, now fifteen had traveled the Atlantic alone, but she was safe. With her arrival, the siblings of Lekka grew stronger in the new world, their shared goal unwavering. Their mission was one, to save, in order to reunite the whole family. Even if Father held the reins from afar, they would pull their weight here, day by day, hour by hour and step by step.

There was laughter now, real, rolling, boisterous laughter inside the small, drafty apartment on Cartier Street looking across the Jacques Cartier Bridge. Five siblings, Athena, Christina, Maritza, Pavlos and little Anna. Five souls once scattered across lands and sea, now huddled together in the warmth of each others' presence. Every night felt like a celebration. Whatever they ate, even if it was just boiled lentils, warm bread, and milk in chipped glasses, they ate with gratitude. They worked with purpose. They shared one bathroom, two bedrooms, and a single dream, to reunite their family. They vowed to never again be at the mercy of Father's rages, of famine, or of fear. They'd crowd around the small table at dinner, speaking over one another, laughing at Pavlos' tales of learning to clean poultry in a Greek owned butcher shop and giggling when Maritza tried to imitate the Canadian girls she saw on Saint Catherine Street. Christina, ever curious and quiet, would sit listening, observing, always sketching the moment in her mind. Once in a while, Christina couldn't help but blurt out an unexpected joke that made them all laugh wholeheartedly. Athena watched them all and felt a warm swelling in her chest. They were alive, safe, together and they were free, freer than they had ever been under Father's roof. Yet not a night passed when Athena didn't look at the empty space where three chairs might have been. Aphrodite, Eleni and Katerina were missing. They were still in Lekka. Aphrodite and Eleni were the ones who had not come because they had eloped and escaped in a different way. Katerina, the smart one was busy with school, just as Father had instructed.

In her letters, Athena asked about Aphrodite and Eleni. She asked where they were and how they were living, but news was scarce. The war, the pride, and the shame of defiance blurred the lines of communication. Father never spoke their names. Athena knew they had chosen freedom, just like she had, and yet, on cold nights, when the wind howled against the thin walls of their apartment, she missed them terribly. She missed their laughter, their arguments and their singing. She missed knowing with certainty, that they were okay. Still, five candles now burned in the cold Montreal night, and with every flicker of their flames, was a promise lit. They would keep going. They would survive and they would build something better than what they had come from.

Chapter 26: Crossroads of Desire and Devotion

The climb up Mount Royal was steep, but Athena barely noticed the burn in her calves or the winter wind that tugged at her coat. Aristotelis walked beside her, unusually quiet, for once not boasting about his job prospects or his latest dealings with Montreal's bustling Greek business community. There was something different about him tonight, less performance and more presence. The city glittered below like a field of stars scattered by a careless god. It pulsed with possibility. Above them, the great iron cross glowing faintly in the cold, stood sentinel against the dark sky. Athena pulled her scarf tighter around her neck as they stepped onto the overlook.

He turned to her. "You always look like you're carrying the whole world, Athena," he said softly, brushing a curl from her cheek. "Let someone else carry you for a while."

She smiled timidly. "I don't know how to do that."

He stepped closer. "I can show you." His kiss was not rushed or forceful. It was shockingly warm against the winter night, and it was full of intention. Her breath caught. She was stiff with the weight of tradition, of lessons whispered by her mother, and of shame. She resisted. Then her hands found the collar of his coat, clutched it as though afraid to fall, and her lips moved with his. The heat spread from her mouth down through her chest, into her belly, pooling low in her body where she had never before let her thoughts linger. Her knees weakened, her fingers trembled as they slid up into his hair. His hands, strong and sure, held her face, then her waist, then lower, as if asking permission that she could not find the words to grant or deny. His touch was reverent, but confident. He seemed to know her body before she did. He touched it as if he'd always been waiting for it to awaken. She gasped when his hand brushed the curve of her hip and when his mouth trailed to her neck. There was fire in her blood. Her thighs pressed together, her pulse quickened and her skin burned despite the winter wind biting at their exposed faces.

"Athena…" he whispered gently against her ear. "You make me believe in more than just ambition."

She didn't speak. Her thoughts were tangled. Dimitri's memory flickered like a dying candle. She had waited as a good girl should. She had denied her body's longings. She had sacrificed, obeyed, and had given everything she had to everyone else. Now, with this bold, flirtatious, and worldly man whose values so often challenged her own, she felt alive. She shook with the shame of it and trembled with the thrill. Was this sin, or was it life? She pulled back, breathless, her hands pressed against his chest. "I shouldn't…"

His hands fell away, but his eyes did not. "Shouldn't?" he said gently. "Or don't want to?"

Athena looked up at the glowing cross. Her heart pounded and her body screamed, *"Yes, I want to!"* But her conscience and her soul quivered with confusion. She was still bruised by the choices she'd made, by the loss of Dimitri and by Father's demands. She turned from the cross back to Aristotelis to whisper. "I don't know who I am anymore."

He leaned forward, his forehead resting on hers. "Take your time Athena *mou.* (my Athena) Let's find out together."

For days after their night beneath the cross, Athena could still feel Aristotelis' breath on her neck, his fingers tracing paths down her back, awakening places within her that had once felt dormant. The memory of that embrace clung to her skin like an undeniable and intoxicating scent. She had not gone home with him. Her honor, the iron thread that stitched her character from childhood had pulled her back at the edge. What they shared beneath the cold stars had been enough to rattle something foundational. She had now crossed a threshold.

At church, she felt the hymns differently. The music swelled through her body not as comfort, but as a question. Her voice trembled the first time she sang after that night, still pitch perfect, still as angelic as ever, but thinner and unsure. The parishioners didn't notice. They still turned their heads when she walked past with her polished shoes, her small waist and her full bosom, modestly covered. She was still the young woman from Lekka who had made something of herself. She was the girl who translated hospital forms and immigration papers for the old men with dusty hats and the frightened young mothers looking for a better life for their children. Inside her being and her soul, Athena was unraveling a new self.

She sat at her little kitchen table one morning, coffee cooling in her hand, staring at the envelope from Lekka. Her father's firm script scolded her from across the sea, reminding her of her duty, of the land he had foolishly bought, of the children and her three siblings, still waiting and still hungry. Her mother's resigned voice echoed in her head, *"You are the strong one, koritsi mou. 'My girl'. You are the hope."* But what had she done with that hope? She had wanted to fall into Aristotelis like water into parched earth. She had wanted to let go, to stop carrying everyone else's burden for just one night. She longed to be desired, not for her virtue, or her sacrifice, but for her body, her womanhood but mostly, herself.

Guilt gnawed at her. She picked up her comb and ran it through her hair harder than necessary trying to tame the waves that curled with defiance. She stared at herself in the mirror. She had grown more beautiful, more womanly since arriving in Canada. Her cheeks were fuller and her eyes deeper with experience. She didn't look like the girl who once lay on mattresses beside seven siblings, whispering dreams into the dark to drown out the sound of Mother's suffering.

She began avoiding Aristotelis. He would leave messages with friends. His messages showed that he was confused and angry because he didn't understand. He didn't know what it meant to be raised to belong to others, to a family, a village and an iron clad set of rules that were stronger and older than his own desires. Athena missed him. She missed his easy charm, his cleverness and the way he made her feel, but she also feared him. She was petrified of what he had awakened and what she might become if she let go. One evening, she stayed behind after choir practice. She confided in Father Marcus with lowered eyes. "I am changing," she said simply.

He looked at her with gentle eyes. "God made you a woman Athena, not a stone."

"I feel things I shouldn't."

"You feel what is human."

"But I almost..." She stopped, blushing.

"You almost loved someone," he said quietly. "It is not a sin to want love. It is only a sin to forget who you are in the process."

She looked away, ashamed of the longing that still tugged at her belly when she thought of Aristotelis' mouth on hers.

"Athena," he said, "you carry the world on your back. Simon of Cyrene helped bear Christ's suffering by helping Him carry the cross. You don't have to do it all alone."

Athena nodded as comfort gradually enrobed her face.

She wept then, not for Aristotelis or Dimitri, or even her family, but for herself and her realization. She cried for the girl who was caught between duty and desire, between the old world and the new, between tradition and freedom. In the weeks that followed, she sang louder in the choir. The tremble disappeared from her voice, replaced by a new, richer and fuller depth, as if some truth within her had taken root. She didn't avoid Aristotelis but she did not return to that place beneath the cross. She started taking longer walks with him again, to dream and to allow herself to imagine a life that was not only for others, but for herself too. Montreal's Greek community buzzed in whispers, laughter, and stolen glances, especially when Aristotelis entered a room. He had a way of commanding attention without trying. With his crisp suits, thick lashes, and a charming shadow of a smirk always playing on his lips, he seemed to carry the Ionian sunlight with him, even in winter. The women noticed him. Athena saw them staring.

At first, she pretended not to care. She would smile politely at gatherings while Aristotelis charmed the room, watching the younger girls flutter around him like moths to a flame. They tossed their hair, laughed loudly at his jokes, and leaned in close hoping to catch some part of him. She noticed how he let them. It was subtle, just enough attention to keep them hooked. It was never enough to be accused of impropriety. Athena could see the way his eyes lingered, even while he stood beside her. She could feel the heat rise under her skin, tight in her chest and prickling at the back of her neck. Was this what love meant? To ache with insecurity? She had worked too hard for too long to feel this powerless. Her days were filled with service to others, to her family and to the church. She was admired for her goodness, her generosity, her strength, but none of that made her immune to jealousy. When she saw Kiriaki Moustakos, a younger girl with painted lips and expensive shoes giggling at Aristotelis' jokes, her stomach turned. When she caught a glimpse of him offering his arm to another woman at the dance, she felt something cold and sour beneath her ribs, and he noticed.

"Ti sou ftaiei, Athinoula?" (What is bothering you, Athinoula) he asked one evening as they walked the lamp lit streets after a party. "What's wrong, my little Athena?"

"Nothing," she said.

"You haven't smiled all night. You barely looked at me."

"I looked," she said quietly. "So did every other woman in the room."

He stopped walking and turned to face her. "Are you jealous?"

"No," she lied, folding her arms tight across her chest. "Should I be?"

His smile softened, becoming something tender. "You know I want you."

"I don't know anything anymore," she whispered. "I know what I'm supposed to be, what I'm supposed to do and what I've been raised to believe."

He reached for her, holding her hands with a strong, convincing grip. "You're my woman Athena, the only woman for me. Nobody can ever replace you in my heart."

The wind rustled her coat. He leaned in slowly, as though giving her time to turn away. She didn't. When his lips met hers, the world stilled. It wasn't the gentle kiss she remembered from Dimitri. It was not like the kiss under the cross either. This was fire, consuming and breathtaking. Her body responded before her mind could interfere. She clung to him and let herself be kissed like a starving woman. When his hands moved to her waist, she didn't stop him. When they slid lower, she gasped, but didn't pull away. His breath was hot in her ear. "Come home with me."

She froze and for a split second and she considered it. Her body screamed yes. Her heart beat loud enough to drown out the voice in her head, but that voice, that stubborn, ancestral voice, could not be silenced.

"No," she said, breathless, her eyes wide.

"Athena?"

"I can't," she said. "I'm not ready."

He stepped back, ran a hand through his hair, frustrated. "You keep me at a distance, but you don't want anyone else near me either. What is this?"

"It's me," she said. "It's how I was raised. It's what I believe."

His jaw was tense. He looked at her long and hard. "You know that you are the only woman for me and I will wait for you. As long as it takes, I will wait until you are ready."

They walked in silence after that, side by side, but miles apart. That night, Athena lay awake in bed, curled into herself. She hated the part of her that yearned for him, and that vivid, imagined heat of his body beside hers. She hated the other part of herself more, the one that had let jealousy gnaw at her like a feral dog. She wondered if she had made a mistake with Dimitri. If maybe she had been too rigid and old fashioned. She had never even kissed Dimitri the way she kissed Aristotelis tonight. Would things have been different if she had? Tears slipped silently down her cheeks. Her pillow grew wet with longing and shame.

The next day, she rose before dawn and went to church. The doors were still closed, but she sat on the stone steps, clutching her coat around her. As the sun rose behind the steeple, the cross cast a shadow over her. She whispered a prayer, *God, help me choose right. Help me find balance. Help me be enough.* And from somewhere deep inside, a quiet answer echoed, *You are already enough.*

Chapter 27: A Promise and Double Vows

The city hummed with spring. It melted through the alleys of Pine Avenue and lifted the heavy gray from Montreal's shoulders. The snow had receded, the air had softened, and tiny buds unfurled in the neglected branches of old trees. Even the Greek bakery on Roy Street seemed brighter with the scent of honey drenched galaktoboureko floating far into the streets.

Athena had just stepped out of Father Marcus' parish hall, arms full of donated clothing she was organizing for a new family from Thessaloniki when she saw him. Aristotelis was leaning against the gate wearing his effortless crooked smile and that brilliant spark behind his eyes. She hadn't seen him in days, not since the night she told him no.

"You look like a woman with the weight of the world on her shoulders," he said, standing tall, his coat fluttering open just enough to reveal the little, green velvet box in his pocket.

"I'm always carrying something," she replied, the corner of her lips revealing a tiny smile while her eyes narrowed suspiciously.

He stepped forward. "Then let me carry the rest of it." Before she could answer, he dropped to one knee, right there in the street, under the wide April sky. "Athena *mou*," he said, "I want to build a life with you. I want your kindness in my home, your voice in my ears, and your stubborn, magnificent strength in my corner. You're the only woman who makes me feel like I could be more than I am."

Pedestrians paused. Someone gasped. Another whispered, "Look! A proposal!"

Athena blinked. Her hands shook slightly beneath the stack of worn cardigans and winter boots.

"Marry me," he said softly, "and I'll give you a life full of love, laughter and prosperity. I promise."

The world stilled. She wanted to say yes. She also wanted to say, *But what if I'm not enough to hold you still?* She wanted to say, *I don't trust how women look at you, or how you sometimes look back.*

She wanted to say, *I'm scared. I've always been scared of you. You bring out in me something I never knew existed, something I've longed to feel, but have never allowed myself to.* But the only thing she said, in a small but clear voice was, "Yes."

There was applause from the sidewalk. Someone whistled, and someone else shouted, "Congratulations!"

He stood, then he slid the thin, traditional gold ring onto her finger. She had never imagined anything extravagant, but the circle shimmered like a promise under the sun. He kissed her, and though the kiss was sweet, her heart thudded with more questions than answers.

They celebrated quietly. A dinner at a friend's home. A bottle of retsina, some lamb cooked with lemon and oregano. Aristotelis toasted her with a grin. "To my bride, and to the luckiest man in Montreal." Athena smiled, but behind her eyes, doubt wavered. He was still flirtatious and still a charmer. She saw it when they went to the Greek club downtown. Women still leaned in close. Some even glanced at her ring, then back at him as if to say, *That won't stop me.* She saw how he liked being wanted. Still, he called her *kardia mou.* (my heart) He left her love notes written on napkins and told her she was his whole world. Maybe he meant it, but that's not what scared her most. It was too late. She wanted him and she wanted to feel like a woman. She had fallen in love with him, his charm, ambition and his graceful, dangerous ways.

She prayed more often. Spoke with Father Marcus, who looked at her with kind eyes and said gently, "Marriage, my child, is not a cure for fear. It's a partnership in which you learn to carry fear together." One evening, under the quiet glow of the oil lamp beside her bed, Athena stared at the ring on her finger. The gold caught the light like a whisper of something new. She touched it lightly imagining a future that hadn't yet arrived, perhaps with children, laughter, a kitchen filled with music, food and warmth. She thought of Dimitri, only once, not with longing, but with a softened grief of *what if.*

Aristotelis knocked on her door that night. He brought kourabiethes from the bakery. When she opened the door, standing there in her robe, her curls still damp from her bath, he kissed her forehead and whispered, "You'll never regret saying yes to me." Even if she wasn't sure yet, if the ghosts of her past still stirred sometimes, she found herself wanting to believe him.

Soon after, Evangelos appeared to steal Christina's heart. She met him one rainy Sunday morning after liturgy in the church hall where the faithful gathered for coffee, koulourakia and quiet gossip. He was from Rhodes and newly arrived in Montreal, just two months earlier. His accent was musical and his manners impeccable. He was devout, respectful, and full of curiosity. He spoke to Christina not as though she were a prize to be claimed, but as though he genuinely saw her. He admired her softness, her laughter and her care for others. He asked her about Lekka, about her family and her favorite hymns from the choir. By the third Sunday, he brought her a small bouquet of wildflowers he had found at the edge of Parc Lafontaine. Christina blushed furiously but didn't refuse them. A few weeks later, under the trees on Mount Royal, he told her he loved her and asked for her hand in marriage. Christina was breathless and overwhelmed with joy. She had never imagined someone would see her, the quiet middle sister. She had never felt worthy of such love.

When Christina told Athena, her sister embraced her with tears in her eyes. "He's good," Athena whispered. "I can feel it. Do you want to marry him?"

Christina answered, "Yes, Athena! I love him."

"Then let's have a double wedding. It will cost less and we can celebrate our special day together."

"That's a great idea!" Christina whaled. "I will speak with Evangelos."

"And I will speak with Aristotelis and Father Marcus."

The day of the wedding dawned clear and brilliant, with the golden July sun spilling warmth across the rooftops of Montreal. The bells of the Greek Orthodox Holy Trinity Church rang with a joyous urgency, calling the faithful and the curious to witness what the parish had started to call the wedding of the year, two sisters, two grooms and one celebration.

Athena stood before the full length mirror in the church basement, adjusting the delicate veil over her dark, glossy curls which were pinned and swept back elegantly. Her white satin dress clung to her small waist and curved softly over her full bosom. It was a modest gown, yet it was undeniably graceful. There was a quiet glow about her, something noble, mature and almost holy.

Christina, beside her, was radiant in her own gown, her fine features blushing with the excitement of love and youth. Her long, straight, brown hair flowed like silk over her shoulders. She had never looked so alive. Her dark brown eyes sparkled as she nervously toyed with the gold chain around her neck, the one Evangelos had gifted her when he proposed. Maritza, not yet married, helped spread their veils and smooth the hems of their dresses. She joked and teased, her small laughing eyes gleaming, her presence bubbling over with mirth to distract them from their nerves. "You both look like saints," she grinned. "But not too saintly tonight, eh?" Athena rolled her eyes, but even she couldn't help the smile that curved her lips.

The sanctuary upstairs was already full. Every bench was packed with Greek families, immigrants who had come from every corner of the Greece's mainland and islands, Sparta, Roumeli, Kalamata, Samos, Rhodes, Crete, Chios and Kefalonia. There were women in silk scarves, men in dark suits and children squirming and giggling. Many were there out of genuine affection and others out of curiosity. Everyone in the community knew the three sisters, those "good Greek girls" who worked hard, helped newcomers, and always carried themselves with dignity. From the moment they had arrived in Montreal, the sisters had drawn attention from Greek men, handsome bachelors, factory workers, waiters, and shopkeepers, all hoping to find a wife who could cook, clean and bear them sons.

Athena, Maritza, Christina and Anna had been careful. They were raised to guard their virtue and to protect the family name. Their reputation meant everything. One single whisper, a single rumor of being loose or easy, could destroy them. So they walked a careful line. They smiled politely. They danced at church picnics and helped serve food at festivals, but they never let a man walk them home. Even Maritza made sure to never share much more than a dance, polite words and a friendly flirt. There was too much at stake.

The church bells of Holy Trinity rang clear across the grayish blue Montreal sky, echoing through the busy streets. Inside the church, golden light spilled from high windows onto the marble floors, warming the wooden pews, glinting off the polished icons, and illuminating the faces of the gathered guests who waited in reverent silence. Then the doors opened.

Pavlos stood tall at the entrance of the sanctuary, his shoulders straight and his suit crisp and pressed. On either side of him stood his sisters, Athena on his right, Christina on his left. Each bride was dressed in flowing white, their veils trailing behind them like clouds. The brides' arms were linked with their only brother's. Their eyes shimmered with nerves and quiet joy. All three of them were ready to walk down the aisle.

Pavlos had walked many hard roads since he'd come to Canada. He worked long shifts in the butcher shop and had brushed off merchants who sniffed out their foreignness like blood. He made sure food was always on the table, and sometimes, he went without eating. He had been their anchor, their guardian, and now, for one final moment, their father. He blinked hard, swallowing the sudden knot rising in his throat. Father would have wanted this, he told himself. No matter how much bitterness Pavlos held toward the man, he still carried the commandment in his bones, *protect your sisters*. He had obeyed, and here they were, noble, dignified and radiant.

The music swelled, and they walked. As they reached the front of the church, Aristotelis turned, his face softening as he laid eyes on Athena. His hands shook slightly as he took hers, and for a moment, it seemed as if no one else existed. There was genuine admiration in his eyes, the kind that speaks not only of beauty but of deep respect. Athena, who had weathered so much, seemed to stand taller under his gaze. She seemed stronger, prouder and more herself.

Next to them, Evangelos could not take his eyes off Christina. She looked luminous with a quiet smile on her lip. He beamed with boyish pride as he reached for her. Christina's cheeks flushed pink beneath her veil, and she gave Pavlos one last look, half grateful, half tearful before she let go of her brother's arm. Both grooms kissed Pavlos' hand with gratitude, bowing before him with heartfelt tradition and respect.

The ceremony unfolded like a dream with incense curling into the rafters and chants echoing like something eternal. Pavlos stood to the side with his hands clasped in front of him. This moment, this sacred right of passage, was both an ending and a beginning. The peace of the moment was briefly pierced by the sound of unrestrained and bold laughter. It was Maritza, her hair tumbling down her shoulders in unruly waves.

Athena with Aristotelis and Christina with Evangelos stood before the priest, Father Marcus. The double ceremony was filled with the aroma of incense and solemn beauty. Wreaths were placed upon their heads. The candles flickered and glowed. The choir sang in reverence. As their voices rose, so too did the smiles of every man and woman present. Athena glanced at Aristotelis, debonair in his suit and a subtle yet genuine grin on his lips. She felt a blend of affection and uncertainty. She loved him dearly but he challenged her. He made her feel alive, but deep in her heart, she remained concerned with how much of himself he would give and how far his flirtations might wander. Christina, on the other hand, gazed at Evangelos like the earth itself had stilled. She had found her home in his arms. When the priest blessed the unions and the congregation cried *"Na Zeisete!"* (May you now live) the couples were showered with rice, cheers, and ululations of joy.

At the church basement reception hall that night, tables overflowed with roast lamb, stuffed vine leaves, and honey soaked desserts. There was laughter, dancing and music. Christina and Evangelos barely let go of each other's hands. Athena sat with other choir members, sipping wine, watching the older women dance the syrtaki with gusto and flair. Maritza led a line of younger girls in the circle dance, the kalamatiano, her hips swaying and her long black hair bouncing with every step. Athena looked at her family, whole for now, and happy. Even though the road had been hard, and her future with Aristotelis seemed uncertain, Athena allowed herself, for one night, to feel peace.

Later, Maritza danced with abandon, twirling alone in the center of the floor, her skirt flying, her laughter echoing louder than the music. She drank wine, flirted, and threw her arms around both brides much too often. Pavlos watched her from a corner. His brow furrowed and the lines around his mouth deepened. Something in Maritza's wildness unsettled him. She was free in a way Athena and Christina never dared to be, and while part of him admired it, another part feared it. Pavlos knew that freedom could sometimes burn too hot. It could take her places where he couldn't protect her from. His eyes caught hers once, and she winked. Pavlos let out a helpless sigh and shook his head side to side. Today was not a day for worrying he thought. It was a day for blessings, for new beginnings, for two noble women stepping into futures they had carved with unbreakable wills. Pavlos lifted his glass during the first toast and spoke only one line, "To my sisters Athena and Christina. May you be loved as deeply as you deserve, and may you continue to have the respect you have rightfully earned." The room erupted in applause. Athena saw the shimmer in her brother's eyes and in that moment, she knew that no matter how far they had come, Pavlos would always carry their childhood like a torch. Tonight, that torch had become a crown and Athena's heart was overwhelmed with pride.

Chapter 28: A Ticket for Father

It had taken a few months and each sibling had played their part, Athena, Maritza, Christina, Pavlos, and little Anna, each one giving up luxuries, treats, and rest, determined to scrape together the money for another ticket to Canada. Even Athena's new husband Aristotelis and brother in law Evangelos had contributed. Money was collected much more quickly now that they were seven. They quickly collected one hundred and forty-three dollars.

This time, there was no question and no debate to be had. Father had decided that he would be the next to come to Montreal. Athena received the news in a letter from a quiet woman who often acted as the village's unofficial messenger, a neighbor back in Lekka. The letter said little, only that the money had arrived and Father had made arrangements to leave. He would take the ferry to Piraeus. From there, the Nea Hellas would carry him across the Atlantic to Pier 21 in Halifax. Then, he was to take the train to Montreal. The ticket had been bought and there was no turning back.

Athena felt a sudden panic, dropping the letter on the floor. Her heart beat faster than she had ever felt. How would she face Father again? What would she say about the day he spat at her feet? What could she tell him about his blasphemy and the torment she felt in his home? Would she tell Father that his curse of unsettled dust had haunted her across the oceans? Athena could feel the blood rushing to her head. Her cheeks burned red with emotion. She sat at the kitchen table of their small apartment, a pot of lentils simmering on the stove. The air smelled faintly of roasted onions. She stared at the letter on the floor and felt unable to even lean down to go pick it up. Aristotelis watched his wife from the doorway, his jacket slung carelessly over one shoulder while a cigarette dangled from his lips. He slowly walked over to her.

"He's coming!" She blurted nervously. "Father is coming next. What will I say to him? What will I do? I can't tell him not to come. How he will react? I just can't..."

Aristotelis interrupted. He leaned in to hug her. "He's your father *kardia mou.* (my heart)" Aristotelis whispered tenderly, exhaling smoke toward the cracked window as he spoke. "Calm yourself Athena. I'm here. Nobody will ever hurt you again."

"I don't know." She answered.

"You're trembling like he's a ghost. You mustn't fear him. He is now coming into our home. I am sure he will act accordingly."

She didn't respond, instead, her eyes drifted to the chipped ceramic cup in her hands, the one she always drank from when she needed to think. It was the same one she'd clutched the night Dimitri's last letter had arrived, the same cup she held when she received news of Persefoni's disappearance and the possibility of having two more siblings. The cup had become a kind of talisman that grounded her.

"I saw him last in Lekka square," she whispered. "Do you remember what I told you? Do you remember the curse? The names he called me? The ridicule?"

Aristotelis nodded. He knew the story of how Father had flown into a rage in front of half the village and how he'd called her a whore while spitting into the dust at her feet.

"He never came to say goodbye," she added in a calm voice, her lip shaking. "He didn't even walk me to the port. Now, he's coming here. To our home, and I don't know if I want to open the door."

Aristotelis took a slow puff of his cigarette, thinking carefully before speaking.

"You're not a girl anymore, Athena. You're not in Lekka. You are a married woman, a woman with a job, and a voice people respect. You are a woman who stood in front of a queen and brought a man out of prison. If he brings you shame again, I'll show him to the door myself."

Athena's eyes filled with something wet and unspoken. She didn't really need protection, but it did matter that her husband had offered it. Still, the days that followed were uneasy. The siblings prepared the apartment, rearranged furniture, moved the mattresses so that Father could have the newest and most comfortable one. Pavlos scrubbed the floor with such force the splinters from the wood began to emerge. Maritza cooked large pots of fasolada and giggled nervously when she burned the first batch. Christina hung clean curtains and brought an old armchair from a Greek friend that lived on St Denis Street.

The preparation for Father's arrival reminded Athena of those long, tense days in Lekka when the sun beat down on the dry earth and the air was thick with dust. She remembered her siblings taking turns, staking out the rocky walkway that twisted down the hillside into the village square. They knew the rhythm of Father's boots before they could see him, the way the stones shifted under his weight, the impatient stride that always gave him away. From their lookout near the fig tree, they'd crouch low in the tall grass, eyes fixed on the bend in the path. The moment they caught sight of his outline, shoulders hunched, hands swinging hard at his sides, they would scatter like birds, running across the walkway, shouting, "Mother! He's coming!"

Inside their little stone house, flour covered hands would freeze in mid air. Conversations would drop into silence. Laughter would die out. Mother would wipe her hands on her apron, straighten her back, and brace herself. The air would grow heavy, as if the very walls of the home held their breath. Athena remembered it vividly, not just the watching and warning, but the feeling that came with it. She felt the same way now, the sharp thud of her heart against her ribs, the dry taste of fear in her mouth, the cold knowledge that their safety and everyone's peace rested in how quickly they could prepare for his presence. In their home it was a child's first training in vigilance, a quiet kind of war. And now, years later, that same instinct stirred in their bones. They were preparing, alert and cautious, expecting Father to arrive.

Athena moved through it all like a woman underwater. Each step she took toward preparing for Father's arrival only stirred the sediment of memory deeper in her chest. She remembered how he used to talk down to Mother, as if she were less than the dirt on his sandals. She cringed when he said, "Boys bring honor. Girls bring burden." She thought of how he laughed with Persefoni at nights while Mother sat bruised, weeping in secret. She remember when he had squandered the first money Athena sent, not for food, not for schoolbooks, not for medicine, but for land that no one wanted, far out in the forest's hills. Being the owner of *Mouria* and *Kouknoi* meant he was a man of worth. She thought of how he used to lift his head just a little higher to praise Pavlos, never once thanking Athena for the sacrifices she had made. She did not hate her father, but she did not like him and she feared him.

On the morning of his arrival, the siblings stood at *Gare Centrale* (Central Station) watching the passengers step off the train from Halifax. The air was thick with steam and coal smoke. Greek, Italian, Hungarian, and Polish families bustled all around them, holding signs while searching for familiar eyes. And then they saw him. He was thinner than Athena remembered. His hair had grown gray at the temples. He wore a brown jacket over a beige shirt, and his eyes looked like he hadn't slept in days. His presence was almost the same, upright, proud, and cold, but now, he seemed more frail and much less paramount. For a long moment, he said nothing, he just looked at his five children lined up before him and examined his new sons-in-law from top to bottom. His gaze softened as he nodded toward Pavlos and reached to shake his hand. "A real man now," he said. He looked over at the girls. His eyes lingered on Athena. "You're all grown," he said quietly. "You've done well."

Athena nodded, and for the first time, she felt tenderhearted in Father's presence. She was not expecting what she had just heard but she did want him to say much more. She felt worthy of more praise and still ached for Father's blessing. Athena wanted to say so much more, *You are selfish, cruel, and heartless. You have never once given me your blessing. Where were you when we were hungry and when Mother cried? Where were you when I left alone?* but these words remained behind her teeth. Instead, she turned and pointed toward the bags. "Come, Father. Let's go home."

Chapter 29: Lipstick and Lies

The first Sunday Aristotelis missed church Athena told herself it was the snow. The streets were blanketed, and the wind howled down Rue Saint Denis like a pack of wolves. Perhaps he'd stayed in, fallen back asleep, or gone to work early to help a friend. That's what she told herself. It wasn't like him to miss church, not when he knew how much it mattered to her. But then he missed the next Sunday, and the one after that. "Overtime," he said casually, brushing past her in the cramped kitchen. "They need me at the restaurant for night shifts and extra hours. It's good money, *kardia mou.* (my heart)" He kissed her cheek, but his kiss felt rushed and hollow.

She began to notice how he avoided her eyes when he spoke and how he came home after midnight, reeking of cigarettes and wine. His cologne was an unfamiliar scent, too sweet and much too sharp. Some nights, he didn't come home at all. She once asked timidly. "You slept at the restaurant?"

He didn't even flinch. "Yes, there was a shipment and it was too late to come back home. It's easier to just stay there." It wasn't the words that disturbed her. It was the ease of the lie. They had only been married for seven months. Athena remembered her hesitation when Aristotelis proposed. Something in her gut, something had whispered to her that he was not a man to plant roots. He was a drifter, a shadow with a smile. She remembered him looking her in the eye and saying, "I'm tired of running, Athena. I want a life. I want it with you." For that moment, she chose to believe him because she wanted to believe him. She said yes, she wore white and she let herself hope.

Now, she stared at the lipstick stain on his shirt collar. It wasn't red. It was a garish pink, smeared carelessly just below the fold. Athena's own lipstick was always bright red, a shade her mother had once called "the color of defiance." Pink was not her color. She held the shirt in her hands for a long time, standing by the sink as the evening light faded. Outside, the February cold clawed at the windowpanes. Her breath came shallow. There was no denying it. The stain was not hers. She didn't ask him about it. She couldn't. The truth had already answered for him. Instead, she began to watch, closely and quietly.

At church, when he did show up once or twice over the next month, she saw him standing too close to the young women who giggled behind their hymn books. His smile lingered. His eyes wandered. He touched a shoulder and laughed easily with the women. Athena stood beside him, cold and silent, feeling like a shadow of herself. *Was it always like this? Had he always been this man, and had she simply refused to see it?* She remembered the way he spoke when he proposed, the intensity in his gaze. *"With you, I can be something more."* Had she mistaken that hunger for love? Was it her Aristotelis longed for, or was it freedom, security and citizenship? Had he ever truly loved her? Or had she just been the cost of staying in Canada?

These thoughts consumed her. They made her stomach twist, and then, one morning, she vomited. She thought it was stress, grief and anger, but it happened again the next day, and again the day after that. She went to the doctor and when he told her, she did not cry. She didn't react and did not smile. She simply stared at the doctor with blank look on her face, stood up and slowly walked out of the clinic as if in a trance.

Her body had already begun to change. Her breasts were tender. Her sense of smell sharp. Her hunger strange and fleeting. She was going to have a child. She was to have a baby with a man who came home late and kissed her with lies on his breath. Aristotelis was the man who had seduced her with promises and then vanished into the streets of Montreal with other women's lipstick on his collar. The joy she expected to feel, the happiness she had once dreamed of feeling, did not come. There was no swell of warmth and no weeping with gratitude. There was only dread, a quiet, suffocating dread that clung to her skin like cold fog. She placed a hand on her stomach. It was still flat and silent, but inside her, life was forming.

When she got to the apartment, she walked to the bedroom where his shirt still hung on the door. She stared at it and then she slowly pulled it down and stuffed it into the bottom drawer, beneath a pile of socks he never wore. That night, Aristotelis came home after midnight. His hair was slicked back. His boots were muddy and his breath was sour.

"Another long shift?" she asked from the table, where she sat with a cup of chamomile tea.

He looked startled to see her awake. "Yes. Exhausted."

She said nothing. She just watched as he took off his coat and kicked off his boots. He never noticed that she didn't kiss him goodnight, that her chamomile had gone cold hours before, or that her right hand was curled into a fist beneath the table. Days passed. The silence between them grew thick and bitter. Still, he didn't notice, or he didn't care to. Every time she looked at Aristotelis, she remembered Father's voice oozing out of

Persefoni's window in the night. And every time she saw Father walking across the room, she thought of Aristotelis.

She began to hide small bills in a jar beneath the bed. She took extra shifts at Mme. Gagnon's house for spring cleaning and sewing jobs for the church ladies. She told no one. She had no plan, only an instinct of survival. At night, as they lay in bed, he rolled toward her and reached for her hip. She turned away.

"What's wrong?" he murmured.

Athena said nothing.

"You're cold lately," he said.

She nearly laughed. Cold? She had given him warmth, a home, a life. And he had repaid her with absence and betrayal. "I'm tired," she said.

He sighed and rolled away. She stared at the ceiling, wide awake.

Later that week, she went to the Citizen and Immigration office on St. Catherine Street downtown. She asked quiet questions about sponsorship and permanent residency. The woman behind the counter looked at her kindly and told her that with a Canadian wife, Aristotelis would be granted a path to stay. Papers would arrive within the year. Athena nodded, pretending to be a woman proud of her husband's future, but inside, she felt sick. *So*, she thought, *That's it! That's all I was, a key to a locked door.*

She left the office and walked aimlessly through the snow, hands in her coat pockets, the baby quiet and small inside her. She stopped at a bakery window and watched as a couple, their faces close, shared a pastry while laughing. She remembered wanting that once, and believing in it. Now, even the thought of romance felt distant and foolish, like a story told to comfort children. She didn't know what the future held. She only knew that she could not rely on Aristotelis to be faithful, and possibly, not to be the father to her child.

She felt alone again, yet in that solitude, something inside her, a quiet resolve, was awakening. She felt the same strength that had carried her from Lekka to Athens, and then to Montreal. She felt as responsible as when she had helped Mother raise her siblings. That had taught her to endure the cold, the hunger and the loneliness. That strength was rising again. She quickly decided that she would raise this child and she would protect it. She would not let it grow up believing that love came in the shape of betrayal.

When she returned home, Aristotelis was asleep on the couch, shoes still on, snoring softly. She walked past him, went into the bedroom, closed the door, and whispered into the silence, hoping the child could already hear her. "You will be loved," she said. "Even if I have to do it alone."

Chapter 30: Old Wounds

Athena waited until the air between them was still and until the city outside their apartment settled into silence. Once the streetcars stopped rattling and the neighbors stopped shouting in the hallway, she waited until Aristotelis had eaten the stew and bread she had prepared. When he wiped his mouth with the back of his hand like a man who deserved to be spoiled, she still waited, because once she said the words, nothing would be the same.

"I'm pregnant," she said.

He looked up slowly. A moment passed, a brief moment, but enough for her to see the flicker of surprise before it shifted into a smile. Aristotelis' face erupted with a broad, satisfied smile. He sat back in his chair, exhaled loudly, and chuckled. "Bravo," he said. "I knew it." He reached for her hand, squeezing it. "A son, my son, my name will live on!" His voice burst with pride, as if he had won a prize, as if she were nothing more than the vessel that carried his legacy. His eyes sparkled with the thrill of it. Athena smiled even if she had imagined this moment differently.

She wanted a shared awe, tears, a voice whispering, *We're going to be parents,* but this was something else. There was no softness in his joy and no recognition of what it meant for her. No mention of them, just him, his seed, his name, and his legacy. She pulled her hand away slowly. Aristotelis did not notice.

That night, he fell asleep easily. He seemed satisfied. His chest rose and fell steadily beside her. Athena lay awake, her eyes wide open to the darkness. Her body, already beginning to change, felt foreign. She placed a hand over her belly. It was still early and there was no movement yet, only the slow, silent building of life. The child was real, but so was the man she had married. She turned toward the window, her back to him, and bit her lip as a tear escaped her eye.

The next day, Maritza brought a loaf of bread and Christina made lentil soup. They sat at the table in silence for a while, sipping chamomile tea and eating slowly. Athena hadn't told them yet, but somehow, they already knew. Maritza was the first to ask. "You look different. Are you sick?"

Athena looked at her hands. Christina leaned in. "You don't smile anymore. Is it him?" The questions chipped at her, and when Maritza reached over and touched her arm gently, Athena broke.

"I'm pregnant," she said, her voice barely above a whisper.

Christina gasped. *"The mou!"* *'Oh my God!'*

Maritza's eyes widened. "Is it good news?"

Athena shook her head. "I don't know." The silence that followed was thick. "I don't trust him," she said finally. "I never fully did. I see him with other women. He lies. He stays out all night. He comes home with lipstick that isn't mine."

Maritza clenched her jaw. "The bastard."

Christina's face flushed with anger. "You should have said something sooner."

"I was ashamed," Athena whispered.

"You're not the one who should be ashamed," Christina snapped.

Athena looked at them. Her voice shook, "Do you know what I keep thinking about? Mother, and how she used to walk down the streets in Lekka after Father started spending more and more time with Persefoni. I think of how people looked at her, with pity in their eyes and whispers behind their hands. I hated it. And now…" Her sisters sat in stunned silence. "I've become her," Athena said. "I'm carrying the child of a man who doesn't respect me. He does not honor or respect the vows he made to God. And I'm trapped, just like Mother was."

Maritza's voice was soft. "You're not trapped! And you're not her, Athena. You're stronger, so much stronger."

"Then why does this hurt so much?" Athena whispered. "Why do I feel like I'm thirteen again, hearing the neighbors whisper about Father and Persefoni? Why do I feel like a fool? Like I believed in something that was never real?"

Maritza reached for her hand. "Because you wanted to build something better, and now it feels like it's crumbling."

Athena nodded, her voice cracked. "I thought I was saving him and that if I gave him a chance, he would choose to stay. Not only in Montreal, but with me, only with me. Now I wonder if he only married me to stay in the country, and if I was just a passport."

"Do you think he'll leave?" Christina asked.

"No," said Athena. "He's too comfortable. Why would he leave when he has everything he wanted? A wife, a baby, a home and a country he can stay in, legally." She looked at her sisters. "But he isn't really mine. He has everything here in our home, and he's getting everything he wants outside our home as well."

The three of them sat in silence, old wounds reopening. Their father's affair had carved scars into each of them in different ways, but Athena had always carried them the deepest. "I don't want this child to feel what I felt," Athena said. "To grow up in a home where love is a mask. Where the father is a stranger and where the mother is pretending."

"We'll help you," Maritza said. "You're not alone."

Athena nodded, but the shame burned in her throat. "Father is here," she said. "I don't know how to tell him. He'll see everything. He always does. He'll look at me and know something's wrong."

Christina stood and walked around the table, kneeling beside her. "He'll be proud, Athena. You've done so much. Even if it hurts now, even if your husband disappoints you, you've built a life. He'll see that."

Athena shook her head. "But I'm embarrassed. What will he say when he sees the truth? When he sees I married someone like him? A man who lies. A man who can't be loyal." The words hung in the air like smoke. None of them had ever said out loud that their father had failed them. That his betrayal had shaped them in ways they were only now beginning to understand. But it was the truth and it was no longer unspoken.

"You didn't marry Father," Maritza said. "You married someone who pretended to be better. That's not your fault."

Athena closed her eyes. She remembered her mother's face, how it changed after the affair with Pesefoni started, not broken, just hollow and quiet in a way that never went away. And now, Athena felt that quiet sinking into her bones. But she wouldn't let it take her completely. She looked at her sisters. "I'll tell him. I'll tell Father the truth this evening. And I'll raise this child with honesty, even if it's hard and even if it breaks me."

Christina wrapped her arms around her. "You won't break. You can never break! You are Athena!" Maritza joined the embrace. "You're an anchor. You always have been."

For the first time in weeks, Athena allowed herself to cry. Not just tears of anger or grief, but release. The child inside her was still so small, so unformed, but already, it had changed everything. She would not become her mother. She would not pretend, and Aristotelis would soon learn that a wife was not a door to walk through. She was the house itself, and this house, she decided, would not fall, not with her in it.

Chapter 31: Parting for Peace

The days in the Cartier Street apartment grew darker as autumn pressed in. The walls seemed narrower. The sounds of the neighbors seemed louder. Athena moved through the narrow hallway like a phantom, her thoughts harder to shake, growing heavier by the minute. She often caught herself staring at the mirror wondering if she was looking at her own mother. She questioned if her reflection even resembled the woman who first arrived in Montreal. She had come to Canada with hope packed into her bag and now all she saw was shame, pain and resentment. It wasn't just the long stares or the way her voice had become quieter, it was the bitterness in her chest and her fists that clenched at night. It was the way she washed dishes harder than she needed to, as though the clatter might distract her from the rage. She remembered her mother walking through Lekka, expressionless, the hem of her dress catching dust as she made her way past Persefoni's house. Mother's jaw was locked but she still tried to hold her head up high. Athena used to admire Mother's strength although she pitied her. Now she understood that Mother's silence wasn't strength. It was resignation.

Worse still was the fear that she wasn't just turning into her mother, she was becoming her father as well. She was bitter, dismissive and quick to temper. She caught herself cursing under her breath. She slammed the cupboard doors hard and jumped when the dishes inside clattered against each other. She threw plates that shattered against the floor only to fall to her knees to clean them up, sobbing and clutching her belly. She cursed Aristotelis aloud now, she cursed his name. Cursed the day she met him and cursed the ship that brought him to Montreal. The sharpness of her words cut deeper than she expected. Her voice was hoarser and twisted now. It reminded her of the man she loved but disliked the most. She saw Father in herself now. She remembered those dark nights in Lekka when he'd drink too much and throw his anger across the room. Now, she hated the sound of her own voice more than she hated Father's.

The tension spread through the apartment like smoke. Her sisters barely stayed for coffee anymore. Maritza, who once sang while folding laundry, moved quietly through the flat. Christina, normally quick to challenge Athena, had started to avoid her eyes. Her brother-in-law Evangelos grumbled constantly about the cramped space, about the noise and about the way Athena scowled when Aristotelis walked in the door. No one spoke openly about the conflict, but it filled the rooms like steam. Every breath tasted of resentment, and every smile seemed forced. One morning, after another sleepless night filled with slamming doors and muffled arguments, Maritza took Athena aside. "We're moving." She said.

Athena stared at her. "Where?"

"A farm outside the city. There's work there. Room for everyone. Quiet."

Athena blinked to avoid showing her tears. The silence between them swelled. Christina came into the room holding her coat. "We need peace, Athena." And just like that, they were all gone, her siblings, Father and Evangelos. The warmth of shared meals, the laughter, even if dimmed, was gone. The apartment, once too small for so many, suddenly felt vast, empty and cold. Only she and Aristotelis remained. She told herself that this was good and that she wanted to be alone. She thought that perhaps, the peace would help her think.

"You used me." She told Aristotelis the next morning.

He stared at her, dumbfounded. "Why are you talking like this?"

She laughed bitterly. "Because I'm tired of pretending. I'm tired of carrying a child for a man who lies and I am tired of being a mother before I even felt like a wife." He raised his hands in frustration, but said nothing. He knew better. Her rage was not something he could outrun.

Later that night, Athena sat by the window wrapped in a blanket while light snow drifted past the glass like ash. Her thoughts spun in circles. They spiraled back to Lekka, to that dreadful day in the village square when Father cursed her in front of all the villagers, spitting words from the depths of his fractured ego. His words echoed repeatedly in her mind. *"May the shame, sweat, and the swirling of dust swallow your every step! Curse on you, Athena!"* She had never forgotten those words. She had tried to dismiss them as fury, as the wound of a father losing control, but now, as she looked at her own life, she wondered. Had his curses damned her life? Was this why every decision she made felt poisoned? Why love turned into betrayal? Why home became exile? She remembered how the dust rose around her that day, how it clung to her skin and how she had walked away, ridiculed and quivering inside.

Now, she wondered if that dust had never truly settled. Had it followed her across the oceans, clinging to her heels, swallowing each step she took? Did Father's curse take over her life? Was she a woman bound by this curse? Tears filled her eyes. She didn't wipe them away. *Let them fall*, she thought. Let them carve a path down my cheeks so I can feel something other than rage. She placed one hand on her belly. "You deserve more," she whispered. "More than a broken mother and more than a bitter home." She didn't know how she would give that to her baby. She didn't even know if it was possible. Those words felt like a seed in frozen ground. She could not erase Father's curse, but maybe she could end it with her faith, determination and strength.

In the distance, a siren wailed. The street below shimmered with frost. Aristotelis slept behind her. She could hear his breath, even and relaxed. She wanted to scream, but she did not. Instead, she would dream, not of love, but of freedom and of a life where her child would walk streets without shame. She yearned for a life where dust would not follow her every step and where the swirling of past wrongs would dissolve into the light of something new.

She closed her eyes and prayed. She did not pray to be saved, but to be strong enough to save herself and her unborn child.

Chapter 32: The Price of Promises

The winter thaw came slowly to Montreal, but something in Aristotelis began to warm as the snow receded. He spoke more often of dreams, of purpose and of the future. One evening, he burst into the apartment with a folded piece of paper, his eyes alive in a way Athena hadn't seen in months. "Come," he said, grabbing her hand. "I want to show you something."

They walked south from Cartier to Ontario Street. The air still held a bite, but Aristotelis walked quickly, pulling her along the slushy sidewalk until they reached a small storefront, its sign dusty and its windows covered in old newspapers.

"What is this?" Athena asked.

"Our future," he said. "It's a deli. Or it will be. It's mine, ours."

Inside, the place smelled of old meat. The tiles were cracked. The walls were stained, but Aristotelis looked around with pride. "A man from Kefalonia owns it. His name is Spiros. He wants to go back home to retire. He's letting me buy it in payments, month by month. He believes in me."

Athena's arms were crossed, her belly rounding. She looked around, uncertain. "And you have the money for this?"

"I will. We will," he said. "We'll work together, side by side. You won't have to worry about me staying out late, no other women. You'll be with me, always."

She didn't answer. But something inside her softened at the idea of purpose. She entertained the idea of working for something real, together, beside her husband and of not being left behind.

They opened two months later. The sign read *Delices d'Hellas* (Hellenic Delights) in a bold, uneven script. The neighborhood was rough around the edges, but busy and hungry. The deli now smelled of oregano, lemon, and sweet onions. Athena began to learn how to slice pastrami, smoked meat and serve souvlaki. She already knew how to count change and clean grease from her apron. Her life in Montreal had taught her. At first, it felt good. It was real. She almost believed him. Aristotelis beamed when he wore his apron, his sleeves rolled up, calling customers *mon ami* (my friend), and slicing meat like an artist. He flirted still, he couldn't help himself, but now Athena was beside him. She could see it, interrupt it and control it, but the doubt never left.

Late one evening, Athena sat at the counter, legs swollen, wiping surfaces for the third time. Aristotelis counted bills behind her.

"We'll be known," he said. "Give it a year and people will say, *That's the best Greek food in Montreal.*"

She looked at him and smiled weakly. "And then what?"

He looked confused. "What do you mean?"

"When we're successful, when we have money, will I still be beside you? Or will you leave me behind again?"

He turned cold. "You're always doubting. I brought you into this Athena. You are my wife, the mother of our baby. You have nothing to fear." But fear didn't listen to reason. It sat in her stomach, curled next to the baby growing there.

When Father had arrived from Greece, she had expected a confrontation, a war, a settling of past conflict, defiance and resentment. That did not happen. Now, she needed someone to see her pain and name it. She hoped it might be Father, but she doubted it would be. She found herself once again a daughter without a defender when Father came to visit one evening. They sat on the couch as the dusk settled. Father smoked while his eyes fixed on the skyline from the window.

"*Baba*," she said, "I need to tell you something."

He looked at her, waiting.

"Aristotelis has had other women."

He didn't flinch. "And?"

Her mouth dropped. "And? And I'm his wife!"

Her father waved his hand dismissively. "Men have needs. It's in their blood. They wander, yes, but they return. You will not shame him."

Athena stood, her face hot with disbelief. "So I should be silent, like Mother was?"

Father looked away. "Your mother was strong. She endured."

"Endured?" she whispered, her voice cracking. "You mean she was humiliated. She walked through Lekka trying to keep her head high while everyone whispered about you and Persefoni. I heard them. I remember."

"Your mother had her place," he said. "And you have yours. Act accordingly."

And with those words, the last thread of reverence Athena held for Father snapped. He was not her protector. He was a man of his generation, where honor meant silence for women and freedom for men. How could she have expected a different reaction? She returned to the deli and scrubbed harder, and cleaned deeper as though she could wash the history from her skin. It was too late.

The bitterness had already streamed in, embedded in her very soul.

Each time Aristotelis smiled at a female customer, Athena felt herself recoil. Each night he came home late, even from the deli, she imagined bright and unfamiliar lipstick, staining his collar. She continued to change. She cursed under her breath, loudly sometimes. She didn't recognize her voice anymore. She was harsher and hardened. "God damn it," she hissed one afternoon as she knocked a jar of olives off the shelf that shattered across the floor. "Curse the hands that built this place. Damn the lips that kissed me. Curse the force that brought him here." And then she froze. She finally heard herself. She had become her angry, mean, venom tongued father.

She now stared at Aristotelis not with longing, but with loathing. She resented him and became obsessed with the thought of losing him. She loved him and deserved his loyalty. When she handed him his lunch, it was with clenched fingers. When he kissed her cheek, she stiffened. She had never wanted to be this woman. And yet here she was, her child growing inside her, in a business that bore her sweat, with a husband she could not trust and a father who preached silence and injustice. The mother she had once pitied, was now reflected in every mirror. Worse still, Athena realized that her behavior, her words and her very soul had been taken over by everything she loathed about Father.

Athena stood on the steps of the deli that night. The streets were quieter than usual and the snow was slushy after the day's traffic. She looked up at the pale sky and whispered, "I curse the day I believed him. Damn the day I became a woman to pity. I curse the day I thought love could be enough." The wind shifted, and she prayed. "God, please give me the strength."

Athena placed her hand over her belly and even if she wasn't convinced, "I won't curse you," she said to the life inside her. "I promise to not pass this down." She looked up at the heavens, and whimpered, "God, please help us."

Chapter 33: The Final Arrivals

Spring came to Montreal and the first warm winds of the season stirred the dirty snowbanks. Montreal's skies were still gray, but its streets were bustling as ice gave way to slush. With the thaw, came what Athena had worked years for, the arrival of the rest of her family, all of them, big and small.

Christos was the first to land in Canada. He arrived with tired hands, a rugged pride in his step, and a quiet promise to bring the rest of his family. Weeks later, his wife Eleni followed, her daughter Amalia in her arms. The stunning child turned heads on Saint Laurent with her beauty, and Athena's heart warmed at the sight of her. She looked like something out of a myth, a black haired, blue eyed little goddess amid the gray of the city.

Then came Aphrodite, Dionisios and their four children. Laughter and chaos spilled into Athena's small Cartier Street apartment. Finally, after years of letters, sacrifices, and prayers, Mother arrived with Katerina, the most educated of them all. They flew by plane which was an unimaginable luxury in Lekka. Mother was thinner than Athena remembered. Her shawl was wrapped tight around her shoulders. Her eyes took in the foreign streets with awe. Athena melted into Mother's arms as she approached, like the little girl clinging to her mother for protection and support when in danger. They both cried, sobbing in unison as if they had now become one. Mother pulled away slightly to look into Athena's eyes. Her voice was as gentle and comforting as Athena remembered, "I am so very proud of you Athena!" She then repeated the same words *Yiayia* had often said, "You are the wild fig tree that grows even in stone." With those words as her armor, Athena swiftly wiped her tears with her sleeve. Mother continued, "You are Athena, my beautiful and strong Athena. Do not ever forget that!"

Katerina, was still sharp and wide eyed. She walked through the terminal with books clutched to her chest. "She'll go far," Father had always said. She was the only one besides Pavlos "smart enough, and deserving enough to go to school."

Athena should have felt whole with everyone gathered under one sky. She had finally made it happen. She had scrubbed floors, saved every coin, sacrificed sleep and dignity for this. Now, as she watched her siblings share snacks in the farm kitchen, as laughter echoed off the house's cracked walls, Athena felt a silence inside her that no voice could fill. It should have been joy. It should have been triumph, but all she could feel was a hollow ache.

Aristotelis stood across the room, slicing bread for the children, smiling as though he were the proud patriarch of this little kingdom. Athena watched him, wondering how much of that smile was real and how much was performance. She still woke in the middle of the night, hand on her belly, listening for the creak of the front door. She still checked his shirts for lipstick she didn't wear. She still counted the hours he spent at the deli alone. She often thought of the promise he had made when they bought the deli, that they would be side by side, working together, safe from temptation. The promise felt thinner by the day. Now that everyone was here, and her duty fulfilled, she found herself wondering. *Was duty enough? Was this the prize she had worked for?* A now she had an empty apartment, an unfaithful husband, and a silence in her soul that grew louder with every passing day.

One evening, as they all sat crowded around the table at the farm just outside Quebec, plates of keftedes and bread between them, Athena looked up and found her siblings watching her.

"You don't eat," Eleni said softly.

"I'm tired," Athena replied.

"Are you happy now?" Katerina asked, her voice innocent but piercing.

Athena forced a smile. "I have everything I wanted."

Christos tilted his head, studying her. "Do you?"

She stood and cleared the table before anyone could say more. Later, as she sat alone on the balcony, the sounds of her reunited family humming through the farmhouse, she whispered the truth to the wind. "I thought this would fix everything, but it didn't." Even with her family here, safe and no longer hungry, even with her belly round and her name known in the Greek community, she couldn't quiet the rustling inside her, *This is not the life you dreamed of.* The worst part was that she didn't even know what that dream had been anymore. Was it love? Freedom? Respect? Had she ever wanted more than to be free of fear, hunger, and loneliness? Or had she simply become so skilled at survival that she mistook it for happiness?

She closed her eyes and thought of Lekka, the dust on the roads, the sound of Mother crying in the dark and the whispers that followed them to church. She thought of Father's curse in the square. Had it followed her across the oceans? Had it buried itself in her womb, in the cracks of her marriage, in the shadowed corners of her new life? She pressed her hand to her belly, feeling the small, fluttering life within. The thought of Father's curse *"May your womb dry up like old figs."* filled her soul and took over her entire being.

"I brought them here," she whispered. "I saved them, and still, I feel lost." And though she would never speak it aloud, the thought that haunted her deepest was this, *What was the price of selflessness? Was it too high? How would things have been if she had, just when it truly mattered, put herself first?* She wept quietly, not for the sacrifices made, but for the girl she had once been, the girl who believed that if she worked hard enough, loved deeply enough, gave everything she had, then happiness would come. It hadn't.

Two days later, Athena came home to find Aristotelis in the mirror adjusting the collar of a brand new, navy woolen jacket with sleek, shiny gold buttons. *It's too fine for deli grease* she thought.

"What is that?" she asked, not bothering to hide the irritation in her voice.

"Do you like it?" he turned, grinning. "It was on sale, Italian cut."

Athena crossed her arms over her belly. "We're supposed to be saving, for the business and for the baby."

Aristotelis waved a dismissive hand. "You worry too much. I work hard. I deserve to dress like a man who owns something."

"You own debt," Athena snapped. "We're paying the Kefalonian in monthly installments. The deli isn't even profitable yet. We eat lentils four nights a week so you can buy Italian wool?"

He stepped closer, voice lowering. "I am building a name. People respect men who look like they belong. You want customers? You want us to grow? Let me look the part."

"And what part do I play?" she hissed. "The tired wife? The one who washes rags and pinches pennies while her husband pretends we live in a movie?"

"You're always so angry," Aristotelis muttered, shaking his head. "This isn't Lekka. No one respects a woman who nags."

"I'm not nagging. I'm surviving," Athena bit back. "Maybe if you tried that instead of impressing strangers, we wouldn't argue every day."

He rolled his eyes and turned back to the mirror, smoothing his jacket. "You think this is about clothes. You think small, Athena. I'm trying to build something big."

"I've built everything," she whispered, voice trembling. "And I'm still the one holding it together." For a moment, he said nothing. Then, walking toward her he said, "Don't cry. You're pregnant.

You're very emotional. Everything will be alright. I'll make us successful. You'll see."

She turned away, clenching her fists at her sides. He didn't understand. He never had. With every new shirt, every charm he used on the customers, every woman's laugh that lingered, Athena feared more and more that she was disappearing, not just in his eyes, but in her own. What was she now, if not just another woman left behind while the man pursued his ambition and his needs? She swallowed the rising lump in her throat. The baby kicked gently beneath her ribs, as if reminding her of the real future she carried. She had hoped for partnership. Instead, she felt totally alone.

Chapter 34: She Holds On

Aristotelis had gone home early that night. After closing the deli, even with the biting wind that sliced down Ontario Street, Athena chose to walk. The tips of her fingers were numb, and the cold had crept into her stockings, but she pressed on, her steps deliberate, her back straight. The night was dark and brittle, the sidewalks were quiet, but she refused to pay the fare for the streetcar. A few coins here, a few pennies there, it added up. Besides, what was she saving for now? Her family was finally here. Her sisters were safe and settled. Pavlos was working. Father, Mother, Katerina, and both Aphrodite and Eleni, along with their families were finally in Montreal. Even Maritza had found her footing. But still, Athena could not shake the instinct to guard every cent like it was her last. Maybe it was habit. Maybe it was the echo of Lekka's hunger, of post war nights when every crumb was counted and even hope came rationed. Perhaps it was just who she was and who she was raised to be.

She cradled her purse tightly in the bend of her arm. The thick, black leather was worn smooth. The purse had brass hinges at the

top, with a clasp that clicked shut like a pair of teeth. The handle
was short, stiff with age, designed to rest snugly against the inside
of her elbow. The purse was heavy tonight, stuffed with the day's
cash earnings from the deli and with bills folded and bound with
rubber bands. Several coins clinked softly with each step. As she
turned off Ontario Street and began walking toward Cartier, her
breath misted in the air before her. She glanced once over her
shoulder, a reflex she had never outgrown. The street seemed
deserted. She pulled her coat tighter around her belly, her other
hand brushing instinctively over the small, growing swell beneath
her wool. That's when he grabbed her.

Out of the shadows of a narrow lane between two buildings, a
man lunged. Athena tried to scream, but he had his tobacco
scented hand tightly over her mouth. His strong and sudden arm
was around her chest, just above her belly, yanking her backwards
into the alley. Her feet scraped against the icy pavement, her body
twisting as she tried to resist. One hand clawed at the bricks, the
other clutched the purse like a lifeline.

"Give it here." the man growled, pulling at the bag. She wrenched
her body, twisting away from him, the purse still wedged against
her rib cage. Her shoulder slammed into the wall. Pain flared
down her arm, but she didn't let go. He tried to pry her purse from
her arm, jerking the handle hard enough to snap it, but Athena

held on. She thought of her unborn baby. Her mind screamed not just for herself but for the life inside her. She worried for the baby, the life that hadn't yet taken its first breath.

They struggled, his hands rough, her grip tighter still. She felt the man's hot breath against her cheek and his weight pressing in. And then, "What's going on here?" a voice, deep and sharp, cut through the air like a blade. A flashlight beam snapped into the alley. The attacker froze. It was a security guard, stepping into view with authority in every stride. He was big, tall and his shoulders were broad. She couldn't see his face, but she heard his deep, powerful voice, "Hey!" He howled. "What's going on here?"

Athena heard a grunt under the aggressor's breath, and with a shove, he released her. He bolted past the guard and disappeared into the night. Athena staggered back against the wall, gasping for breath, her hands holding her belly while her forearm still clutched the purse. Her knees buckled, but she did not fall.

"You alright, ma'am?" the guard asked, stepping closer.

She nodded, though her voice was slow to follow. "Yes… yes. I think so." Her coat was scuffed, her hands scraped, but she was safe, and the purse was still in the fold of her arm. That night, Athena walked the rest of the way accompanied by the security guard who saved her. Her heart was still pounding. She had fought. She had held on, but she would not speak of it to anyone, not Pavlos, not Christina, not even Aristotelis. She knew the attack had marked her, not with fear, but with something stronger. It was the same resolve that had carried her across the sea, through poverty and through silence. She would not be taken, not her life, not her child, not even her purse.

Chapter 35: Curses, the Cost of Everything

Athena stood at the deli counter alone, wiping down glass that was already clean. Her hand moved not out of necessity, but to quell the storm inside her chest. She was still shaken by the attack, but chose not to say a word to anyone. Her belly was round and heavy. It pressed against the counter edge.

The baby was due soon. Her nerves were frayed thin and she felt a pulling gnaw below her stomach. She glanced outside the window at the front of the deli to identify the odd noise she was hearing. She saw Aristotelis pulling up outside, the engine purring like a smug, expensive cat. Athena glanced through the window to see a brand new, 1955 Chevrolet Bel Air, sleek, glossy white, with black trim and chrome that sparkled even in the gray light. It glistened like sin on four wheels. It was the kind of car that made heads turn and neighbors whisper. Aristotelis stepped out like a king, beaming with pride. He smoothed the front of his coat and strode inside with the kind of swagger that made Athena's skin crawl.

"You like it?" he asked, arms spread.

She didn't answer. She stared at him, then at the car, then back at him. Her voice, when it came, was weakened but serious. "How much?"

"Two thousand," he said, brushing it off like it was nothing. "But listen, it's a deal. A steal! I couldn't let it pass."

"Two thousand dollars?" Her voice rose now, sharp as broken glass. "Are you insane?"

"Athena," he said, calm and coaxing, "it's an investment. People see this car, they respect you. They think you're successful. It's good for the business."

She could hardly breathe. The stress choked her and her chest and belly were still sore from the attack. "We have a child coming. The deli isn't paid off. We're living week to week, and you…," her voice broke, "you spend two thousand dollars on a car?"

He walked toward her. "Don't do this now, not when you should be proud. This is what men do. We work hard and we show it. I'm building a future for us."

"No," she hissed. "You're building a fantasy for yourself."

He reached for her arm and she pulled back like he'd struck her. "You think this car will fix what's broken between us?" she whispered. "You think people will stop talking because you're driving around in that thing? It only makes you louder. You want applause for ruining the life we're trying to build."

His face hardened. "Ruining it? Athena, you're pregnant, emotional and bitter. That's the problem."

Something inside her snapped. She took a step forward, tears of rage in her eyes, the words tearing from her throat before she could stop them. Then she blurted, *"Na se feroun teseri!"* (May four carry you) The deli went silent, as if even the walls recoiled. Aristotelis stared at her. "What did you say?"

Her hands flew to her mouth, but it was too late. *"Na se feroun teseri"* (May four carry you) a curse and a death wish. These were the kind of words you couldn't take back. They were words that carried weight, like Father's words. They were the type of words that had haunted her since that last day in Lekka. She had promised she would never be like him. She had sworn as a child watching her mother weep in the shadows, that she would never curse with hate, never speak cruelty into the world, but here she was, pregnant, feeling alone in a marriage built on lies. Her lips had conjured a darkness she couldn't contain. "I didn't mean it," she whispered, her voice trembling. "I..."

Aristotelis stepped back from her as if she were made of fire. "Maybe your father cursed you," he said quietly, "but now, you curse yourself, not me." He walked out, the glass door slamming behind him. Then, the car's engine roared like thunder as it peeled away from the curb.

Athena stood still for a long time. The deli felt cold. Her hands, once so sure, now shook as they held her belly. The baby shifted inside her, alive and waiting. She wept, not because he had left, not because of the car, but because she had lost herself. She had crossed into a place she had never wanted to be. She was resentful and angry enough to curse someone she loved. She went home alone that night, moving slowly, mechanically, wiping her swollen eyes with the sleeve of her coat. The Cartier Street apartment was dark. Her siblings were at the farm, with their own families now. Father and Mother were there too. She had never wanted this solitude. Now, it swallowed her whole. She sat on the edge of the bed, staring at the cracked ceiling.

What had it all been for? The sacrifices, the endless work, the years of swallowing pain for the sake of duty, for the dream of a united family, for a marriage that was built on illusion? That's what it was all for? She had given everything. Now, she was angry and blasphemous. As her hands rested on her stomach, she felt a flutter, a strong kick, a protest and a reminder. *There is still life my child*, she promised, *our lives will be untouched by lies, and unshaped by pain.* She would not let herself become like Father, at least not anymore. She would not let her pain teach her child bitterness instead of strength. Right then, she made a promise, another that she did not know if she could keep. She rose from the bed, lit a candle, and stood before the window. She looked at the Virgin Mary icon on the wall. *"Forgive me,"* she whispered to the darkness. *"for becoming what I feared, becoming what I hated, and for forgetting who I was. Please help me no longer be this type of person. God, please help me."*

The wind outside picked up, and somewhere in it, she thought she heard her mother's soft and broken voice. *My kind and strong Athena!* At that moment, she knew then that the future was not yet written for her, nor for her child. Perhaps the swirling dust had never left her. Maybe it had followed her across the oceans, hidden in the folds of her skirt as she stepped off ships? Had it possibly clung to her back in crowded train cars, and sat with her in quiet church pews where she tried to find peace in song? Worst of all, had the curses been planted in the womb where a new life now fluttered? Perhaps she had just kept sweeping the curse aside, thinking the dust would settle, but never had.

Tonight, that dust had risen high. With her own voice, she had become the very thing she had promised never to be. She had spat out a curse like fire, poison and dirt, *"Na se feroun teseri!"* was just as harsh as Father's curse, *"May your womb dry up like old figs,"* She had hurled evil curses that she could not erase. Even Mother's whispers in the wind couldn't erase the words she had spat out at the man she loved.

She clutched her belly as if she could shield the life inside from her own anger, her own bitterness and her own becoming. Maybe the dust had always been inside her. Maybe she had inherited it. Maybe pain and anger were in her blood, passed down like heirlooms from Lekka's narrow streets to Montreal's icy sidewalks. But perhaps she still had time to break the curse that haunted her, that changed her, and held her so tight? It was time to sweep the dust not under the rug, but into the light. It was time to name it, to face it, and to burn it out.

The thought of breaking the curse, of starting over, of forgiving and forgetting felt terrifying. Athena needed to make a decision. She looked out the window at the cold street below, the snow now falling again. The city that had once promised, now looked like a stage of shadows. Something stirred within her. Even if her words were as poisonous as Father's and her fury had grown fangs, she was still herself, Athena, woman of storms, and woman of wisdom, but she was still not the woman of freedom that she dreamed of being. She was still not free from her past nor from the curses.

She reached down and pressed both hands to her belly. The baby kicked, strong and sure. "Maybe we'll start again," she whispered to the child, to the silence and to the ghosts that haunted her. In that moment, there was no resolution and little relief, only the knowing that she had work to do, not for her family, not for Aristotelis, not even for her unborn child, but for herself. God, she knew, was mighty, and He had a plan. She knew that prayers were stronger than words, much more powerful than curses, and more liberating than anger.

And so, Athena did what she always did when she was overwhelmed by suffering, she escaped into the beauty of Lekka. She thought of the sun spilling over the mountains at dawn, and the way the light caught the dew on fig leaves like tiny blessings from above. She saw the olive trees trembling in the wind, and imagined the way the village view from Lekka square opened like a cradle into the Aegean. Her heart ached with the weight of those memories, so distant now it felt like they belonged to someone else. She remembered the sound of goat bells echoing from the hillsides, and the laughter of children running past the well near the village square. From its edge, the mountain dropped steeply, like the spine of a great sleeping beast, and beyond it, the sea shimmered like a glorious and eternal secret. In that remembered beauty, nothing was broken. Nothing was heavy. The sky was always blue, the earth always generous. Athena's thoughts helped her feel whole. There was always beauty, and always something waiting in her memories, ready to numb her pain.

She stood behind the deli counter, her hands moving by instinct. The clang of the streetcar in the distance echoed through the windows, like a bell tolling in another world. She blinked, the image dissolving as the bell above the door jingled. A cold breeze stirred her hair. Then, she felt a warm sensation. When she looked down, a dark, crimson stain spread across her skirt, stark against the pale fabric. Beneath her, a small pool was forming on the worn linoleum floor. The buzz of the deli lights faded, and the world narrowed to the hot wetness between her legs, the low pulse of pain rising. The room tilted slightly. Her hand went to the edge of the counter for balance. She gasped, *"God help me! God please help us!"*

A sharp pressure twisted low in her belly, then another, deeper, like a wave rolling through her. She thought of the baby. Her free hand went to her abdomen, to the quiet swell beneath her apron. A customer at the far end of the store called her name. "Madame Athena?" The sound felt distant and muffled, like it came through water. Her heart thudded like a drum and her breath shadowed by every beat. She looked again at the floor. The blood was still there. It was real, not a vision, nor a memory. Yet, even as panic threatened to rise in her chest, another image took shape in her mind, Maritza dancing barefoot through Lekka square, her skirt twirling in the breeze and Pavlos chasing chickens with a stick. She saw Christina braiding Katerina's hair. She heard Mother's voice singing a lullaby, softly under her breath.

A silent tear slipped down her cheek. She straightened herself just enough to stay standing until help came. Her hands gripped the counter again, firm and steady this time. She wasn't sure if that baby planted inside her was about to blossom, or if it had just begun to wither. Outside, the snow kept falling. Athena pressed her hand gently to her belly, and the unsettled dust of her past, of her choices and of her sacrifices, began to twirl again.

Athena closed her eyes. The bells of Agios Ioannis Prothromos Church resonated loudly in her ears. She put her hand to her heart, bent her head upwards towards the heavens, and prayed. She prayed for her baby. She prayed for Aristotelis and finally, she prayed for herself.